DESPERATE RIDE

The train was almost at a standstill now, just barely creeping along. "Hang on," Ryan warned. "We're getting the hell out of here!"

Jessie tightened her arms around Ryan's waist and pressed herself to him as he dug his heels into the flanks of the big black horse. Lucifer hesitated only an instant before plunging out through the open doorway of the freight car. Behind them, the tied-up bandit screamed lurid curses in Spanish as they left the car.

For a dizzying couple of seconds, Jessie and Ryan were airborne atop Lucifer, then the horse's forehooves hit the ground with the clarion ring of steel against stone. Jessie heard shouts of alarm and twisted her head to look toward the engine. Several of the *bandidos* came pouring off the train, and they were yelling and pointing at the fugitives.

Jessie reached down with her right hand and closed her fingers around the smooth wooden grips of the revolver holstered on that hip. She twisted just enough on Lucifer's back to reach across with the pistol and bring it to bear on the startled outlaws . . .

DON'T MISS THESE
ALL-ACTION WESTERN SERIES
FROM THE BERKLEY PUBLISHING GROUP

THE GUNSMITH by J. R. Roberts
Clint Adams was a legend among lawmen, outlaws, and ladies. They called him . . . the Gunsmith.

LONGARM by Tabor Evans
The popular long-running series about U.S. Deputy Marshal Long—his life, his loves, his fight for justice.

LONE STAR by Wesley Ellis
The blazing adventures of Jessica Starbuck and the martial arts master Ki. Over eight million copies in print.

SLOCUM by Jake Logan
Today's longest-running action Western. John Slocum rides a deadly trail of hot blood and cold steel.

— WESLEY ELLIS —

LONE STAR

AND THE MOUNTAIN OF FIRE

J

JOVE BOOKS, NEW YORK

LONE STAR AND THE MOUNTAIN OF FIRE

A Jove Book / published by arrangement with
the author

PRINTING HISTORY
Jove edition / May 1995

All rights reserved.
Copyright © 1995 by Jove Publications, Inc.
This book may not be reproduced in whole
or in part, by mimeograph or any other means,
without permission. For information address:
The Berkley Publishing Group, 200 Madison Avenue,
New York, New York 10016.

ISBN: 0-515-11613-0

A JOVE BOOK®
Jove Books are published by The Berkley Publishing Group,
200 Madison Avenue, New York, New York 10016.
JOVE and the "J" design are trademarks
belonging to Jove Publications, Inc.

PRINTED IN THE UNITED STATES OF AMERICA

10 9 8 7 6 5 4 3 2 1

Chapter 1

With a rush of footsteps, the killers came out of the dark Mexican night.

Or maybe they weren't killers at all. Maybe they were just thieves, out to rob the man and woman who were—perhaps unwisely—walking through the streets of Monterrey.

Ki didn't care. Anyone who attacked him or Jessie was the same in his mind, and would be dealt with in the same way.

Violently.

Ki launched himself forward, his foot snapping out in a high kick. His rope-soled sandal crashed into the jaw of the first man, flipping him backward. The man sprawled limply on the hard-packed dirt of the street, either out cold or dead.

Before the man even landed, Ki had pivoted, the foot that struck the first blow coming down to support his weight as he spun and kicked out with the other foot, his motions almost too fast for the eye to follow, even if there had been enough light to see clearly. The toe of Ki's foot dug sharply into the belly of the second man, making him grunt and doubling him over in pain. Ki chopped at the back of the man's neck with the side of his hand. The man dropped like a stone.

That left the third man, and he came to a desperate, skidding stop as he heard the unmistakable sound of a gun's hammer being eared back. A stray beam of moonlight glinted on the derringer held rock-steady in Jessie's hand as she leveled it at the third man and said, "That's far enough."

The attacker froze, staring into the over-and-under barrels of the derringer from a distance of about a foot. Ki's hand came down on his shoulder, right where it met the neck, and incredibly strong fingers dug into the man's flesh, seeking the bundles of nerves that Ki knew were there. The man gasped, stiffened, and folded up like a house of cards.

Jessie lowered the derringer and asked, "Is that all of them?"

"It seems to be," Ki replied.

"What the hell was that all about?"

Ki knelt beside one of the fallen men. A match flared into life. Ki held the flame steady, using the harsh glare it cast to study the coarse, bearded features of the unconscious man sprawled in the street. While the match still burned, Ki turned to check the faces of the other two men. Then he shook his head, dropped the match to the street, and ground it out in the dirt.

"I've never seen any of them before, at least not that I remember," he said.

"Neither have I."

Ki's broad shoulders rose and fell in a shrug. "Thieves, assassins, *quien sabe*? Does it matter? They won't trouble us anymore."

"I guess you're right. And I suppose we shouldn't have taken this shortcut to the restaurant. I didn't want to be late for the meeting with Don Arturo, though."

"Don Arturo will wait," Ki said. "He wants to sell Lucifer,

2

and he knows you are willing to pay his price."

"Yes, I suppose you're right." Jessie lowered the hammer of the derringer and tucked the little weapon away in her bag. "Well, let's go."

They started along the narrow street again, leaving the unconscious men where they had fallen, but Jessie glanced over her shoulder as she went. She wished she knew if someone had sent the three men after her and Ki. As far as she knew, she had no enemies here in Monterrey.

But if there was one thing she had learned over the years, it was that enemies could be hiding just about anywhere. . . .

It would not have been an exaggeration to say that every eye turned toward them when they entered the restaurant a little later. It was doubtful that the place had ever seen the likes of Jessica Starbuck and her friend and protector Ki. Jessie was tall and beautiful, her lushly rounded figure displayed to advantage in the expensive gown of dark blue silk she wore tonight. As usual, she wore her lustrous copper-blond hair loose so that it fell in waves around her shoulders. Her green eyes searched the room, looking for the man they had come here to meet.

Ki walked beside her, no hint of subservience in his demeanor even though he had been hired years earlier by Alex Starbuck, Jessie's late father, to protect her and be her companion. Jessie might be the sole owner of the vast Starbuck business empire, but she and Ki were partners in almost everything that really counted. They had faced danger together many times and risked their lives for each other without hesitation.

Ki was half-Japanese, half-American, a tall, broad-shouldered man who wore denim trousers, a black vest, and a collarless white shirt. A black Stetson was on his head. His outfit was typical range garb, except for the rope-

3

soled sandals—and the fact that he didn't wear a gun. He was armed instead with a *tanto,* a short knife with a curved blade that was sheathed inside the waistband of his pants. Also, inside the pockets of his vest were a couple of short knives and a supply of *shuriken,* the deadly little throwing stars that were razor-sharp.

All in all, it came as no surprise that the two visitors from Texas attracted so much attention. They were used to it, but Jessie had never been comfortable with all the staring eyes. She was glad when she spotted Don Arturo Hernandez at a table across the room. The white-haired, distinguished-looking Mexican rancher lifted a hand in greeting.

"Good evening, Don Arturo," Jessie said after she and Ki had made their way around the other tables and crossed the room.

Hernandez stood up and took the hand she extended to him. He bent and kissed it, then held on to her hand as he straightened and said, "Ah, you look even more lovely tonight than usual, Señorita Starbuck! You will make the moon and the stars run away and hide in shame."

"I doubt that," Jessie said dryly. She glanced at the other man who had been sitting at the table with Don Arturo. He was on his feet, too, revealing that he was almost as tall as Ki. The stranger wore the tight brown pants, short jacket, and ruffled shirt of a wealthy ranchero, but he seemed somewhat uncomfortable in the clothes. Not only that, but his thick shock of rumpled red hair and his rough-hewn features made it clear that he was not a Mexican, despite his garb.

Hernandez turned and gestured toward the other man. "Allow me to present my associate, Silencio Ryan."

"Silence O'Ryan," Jessie said as she took the man's hand. "That's an unusual name."

4

"Actually, that's not quite it. The last name's Ryan, and I've been called Silencio ever since I was a kid. That's what my father used to yell for when I was crying. At least, that's the way my mama told the story to me." Ryan grinned, giving his battered features a certain rugged appeal. "Hope you don't mind, ma'am, if I don't kiss your hand like Don Arturo here. That sort of charm comes natural to him, but not to me."

"That's fine, Mr. Ryan. This is my associate, Ki."

Ki and Ryan shook hands. Ki said, "You are involved with Señor Hernandez's ranch?"

"Don Arturo's being too generous when he calls me an associate. I'm his *segundo*."

"The ranch could not function without you, Silencio," Hernandez said. "And that is not being too generous." He waved a hand at the other two chairs at the table. "Please, sit down, my friends. The waiter will bring wine."

As Jessie settled down in her seat, she glanced around at the restaurant. It was undoubtedly the finest in Monterrey, but she would have expected nothing less. Don Arturo owned a large, prosperous hacienda in the nearby Sierra Madre; when he came to town to conduct business, it was only natural that he would select such a lavish place for their meeting.

"Did you have any trouble getting here from the hotel?" Hernandez asked as a red-jacketed waiter hustled up to the table and began pouring wine into their glasses.

Jessie and Ki exchanged the briefest of glances at that question, and then Jessie said, "No, not at all." It seemed highly unlikely that Don Arturo would have had anything to do with the attack on them. After all, Jessie had come here to Monterrey to give him five thousand dollars, and that was a lot of money.

"Good, good." Don Arturo lifted his glass. "A toast, my

friends. To the most magnificent horse in the world. To Lucifer!"

The four glasses clinked together above the table.

Jessie took a sip of her wine and then put her glass down. "You have Lucifer here in Monterrey?" she asked.

"Yes, just as we agreed. By this time tomorrow night, he will be yours."

"Tomorrow night?" Ki repeated.

"Yes. First, there is one last race to run."

Jessie frowned slightly. "You didn't tell me anything about a race, Don Arturo."

"I am so sorry, señorita," Hernandez said smoothly. "I did not know about it until today. But I have been challenged by Esteban Corrales, and I cannot allow such a challenge to go unanswered!"

"Who is this Corrales?" Ki asked.

"A man who has long been jealous of my ranch and the wonderful horses I breed there. He has a hacienda of his own, but he knows it is not the equal of mine, just as his horses are not the equal of mine. Tomorrow, when he pits his champion against my Lucifer, everyone will know the truth. Lucifer will leave Corrales's horse in the dust."

"I'm not sure about having Lucifer run a race just before I buy him," Jessie said dubiously. "What if he was to be injured?"

Hernandez shrugged and spread his hands. "What can I tell you? That horse lives to race. Besides, Señorita Starbuck, what are *you* going to do with him?"

"I'm going to send him to a farm I own in Kentucky and race him," Jessie admitted with a smile. "Eventually, of course, he'll be put out to stud."

"I'll wager old Lucifer is waiting anxiously for that day," Ryan put in with a grin. "No offense, ma'am."

"I grew up on a ranch, Mr. Ryan. None taken." Jessie

6

looked at the big redhead. "I'm curious how an Irishman wound up being the foreman of a ranch in Mexico, though."

"There's not much to the story," Ryan said with a shrug. "My father was a professional soldier. He came over here to Mexico back in the days of Maximilian and Carlota. Some would call him a mercenary, I suppose, a soldier for hire. But once he got here, he fell in love with the land and its people, and he got out of Maximilian's army while he had the chance. He stayed on after the emperor was overthrown and married my mother. My full name is Sean Ramon Alvarez y Garcia Ryan. But like I said, I've been called Silencio ever since I was a sprout."

"Yes, but the name does not suit him," Don Arturo said. "Like every Irishman, he likes to talk."

"And drink?" Jessie asked with a smile.

Ryan lifted his wineglass and smiled back at her. "And drink, among other things. Got to uphold the legacy of the ould sod."

Ki brought the conversation back to business by saying, "We were prepared to arrange the transfer of funds to your bank in the morning, Señor Hernandez."

"The next train bound for Laredo does not leave until the day after tomorrow," Don Arturo pointed out. "We can attend to our transaction following the race tomorrow."

Jessie nodded. "All right. That will be fine, I suppose."

"And after Lucifer has shown everyone how much faster he is than Corrales's nag, you can take possession of him. You have arranged a car for him on the train?"

Again Jessie nodded. "That's right."

"Good. Silencio will accompany you to Laredo, just to make sure that you reach your country safely."

Jessie glanced at Ryan in surprise. "That's not necessary. Ki and I can handle Lucifer."

"I am sure you can," Don Arturo said, "but Lucifer and

Silencio are old friends, and Lucifer has never ridden on a train. I think things will go much easier for you if Silencio is along, at least on the first portion of your journey."

"If the horse is used to Mr. Ryan, it might help to have him along, Jessie," Ki said, although he didn't sound overly enthusiastic about the idea.

"All right," Jessie said. It didn't take much convincing to get her to agree. Silencio Ryan was actually a handsome man, in a craggy sort of way. "If you're sure you can get along without him for that long. You said your ranch couldn't run without him."

"Don Arturo was being generous again," Ryan said. "The ranch will run just fine without me for a week or so."

"*Es verdad.*" Don Arturo rubbed his hands together. "Ah, our food is here."

A couple of the red-jacketed waiters had arrived at the table, each of them carrying a huge platter of food. They began placing the plates on the table. Jessie saw enchiladas, tamales, tortillas so warm that steam still rose from them, beans and rice, and thick stew with chunks of *cabrito* floating in it. Delicious aromas wafted up from the food. Everything looked as good as it smelled.

Don Arturo smiled broadly. "Wonderful food, the company of excellent friends, and a race to be won on the morrow. What more could any man want?"

Judging from the occasional admiring glances she caught Silencio Ryan directing her way, Jessie thought, at least one man at this table wanted plenty more. And she wasn't opposed to the idea at all, at least not in principle.

But she still wished she knew why those three hombres had jumped her and Ki on their way here tonight.

★

Chapter 2

The next day dawned as clear as it ever got around Monterrey, which in addition to serving as the supply point for the ranchers in the Sierra Madre was also the center of Mexico's growing steel industry. The foundries ran day and night, spewing smoke from their tall stacks.

On the outskirts of town, however, in the foothills of the mountains, the air was relatively fresh. The local racecourse was laid out here in a broad valley, and people were already arriving in droves when Jessie and Ki rode up in the carriage they had hired outside the Hotel Condor.

Ki alighted first and turned back to help Jessie, even though he knew perfectly well that she could climb down from a carriage by herself. Old habits were hard to break, however.

He was wearing the same outfit he had worn the previous night, but Jessie was adorned this morning in tight black trousers, a black leather jacket, and a silk shirt of brilliant red. A flat-crowned black hat was perched on her hair, which was pulled back into a loose bun so that the wind could not blow it. Jessie wasn't carrying a bag, so the derringer was riding in its concealed compartment in the back of the wide leather belt she wore.

Low grandstands lined each side of the large oval racecourse, and at least half the seats appeared to be occupied already. Many fine carriages were parked in the field beside the stands. Farther out were the less fancy buggies and wagons, along with saddle horses and plenty of burros with colorful blankets draped over their backs.

"It looks like the whole town turned out for this race," Jessie commented.

"And everyone for quite a few miles around, too," Ki said. "Lucifer's fame must have spread for a long way."

"All the way to the Circle Star in Texas, that's for certain. If I hadn't heard of him there on the ranch, we wouldn't be here now."

Ki took Jessie's arm. "We will find Don Arturo. He must be here somewhere."

Instead it was Silencio Ryan who found them a few minutes later as they made their way through the throngs of spectators gathering for the race. Instead of the *charro* outfit he had worn the night before at the restaurant, he was dressed this morning in faded jeans, a butternut shirt, and a broad-brimmed brown J.B. He lifted a hand in greeting as he spied them through the crowd, then made his way over to them and said, "Morning, Miss Starbuck. Don Arturo sent me to look for you."

"Well, you've found us," Jessie said with a smile. "Where are Don Arturo and Lucifer?"

"Around here at the end of the course. Just follow me."

That wasn't difficult, since Ryan was taller than most of the men in the crowd. The three of them made their way around the long curve of the racecourse until they reached an area of stalls and pens. Quite a few horses were in the stalls, leading Ki to say to Ryan, "I thought Lucifer was racing against only one other horse."

"Oh, these horses are for the other races. Lucifer's running

10

against Corrales's El Rey, but that's not until the last race. There'll be several other races first."

"I didn't know these people went in so much for horse racing. I thought Mexico was the land of the bullfight."

"We love that, too," Ryan replied, his tone implying that the Spanish half of his heritage was just as important to him as the Irish half. "But there's nothing like a good horse race." He pointed. "There's Don Arturo now."

Up ahead, Hernandez was standing beside one of the pens, watching with open admiration on his face as the big black horse on the other side of the fence pranced back and forth in a nervous, high-stepping gait. As Ryan, Jessie, and Ki came up to him, he turned and waved a hand at the animal. "Is he not the most *magnifico* horse you have ever seen, Señorita Starbuck, just as I told you?"

Jessie joined Don Arturo at the fence, resting her hands on one of the rails as she leaned forward to study the horse. "I take it that's Lucifer?"

"But of course! As black as *El Diablo*'s heart, and as fast as the wind!"

Jessie smiled. "He *is* impressive, Don Arturo. But Ki and I haven't seen him run yet."

"You will not be disappointed. This I promise you. Do you think Señorita Starbuck will be disappointed, Silencio?"

"Not hardly," Ryan said.

Ki said, "Who are these men?"

Jessie turned her head to see who Ki was talking about. Several men were walking toward the pen, and in the lead was a medium-size man in expensive clothes. He was followed by an unlikely pair—one man short and broad and sweating heavily despite the coolness of the morning air, the other tall and slender almost to the point of gauntness, with skin so pale as to be nearly colorless. Several hard-faced vaqueros brought up the rear of the little procession.

Under his breath, Don Arturo muttered a curse in Spanish. Then he said quietly to Jessie, "That is the man I spoke of last night: Esteban Corrales. The two with him, the fat one and the one who looks ready to climb into his own grave, are his brothers."

Hernandez stepped forward to greet the men.

Esteban Corrales smiled broadly and said, "Ah, good morning, Don Arturo! A fine morning for a race, is it not?"

"A fine morning to win," Hernandez said.

Corrales laughed. "Which is exactly what I intend to do."

Hernandez snorted in derision and said, "The sun has never dawned on a day when one of your horses could defeat Lucifer, Corrales."

Jessie expected Don Arturo's harsh words to provoke an angry reaction from Corrales. However, the rival rancher merely threw back his head and laughed again. "We shall see about that, Don Arturo," he said. "We shall see." He looked over at Jessie and Ki. "You have guests." Corrales strolled toward them, trailed by his brothers and the vaqueros.

Silencio Ryan leaned over closer to Jessie and whispered, "Better watch this fella, ma'am. He's as slick as boiled okra."

"I think I can take care of myself, Señor Ryan," Jessie whispered back.

Corrales swept off his broad-brimmed sombrero as he came to a stop in front of Jessie. He bowed low, then straightened and said, "Such a lovely woman does me great honor by coming so far to see my horse El Rey win this race."

"How do you know El Rey will win?" Jessie asked. "And how do you know I come from far away, Señor Corrales?"

"Ah, so you know who I am. And as for your questions, señorita . . . I know El Rey will win because I have bred and trained him to always win, and I know you come from another place because there has never been anyone else in this lowly land quite so beautiful as you."

"*Gracias,* Señor Corrales. I suspect, however, that you may be incorrect. Mexico has many señoritas more beautiful than I—and Lucifer is going to win this race."

"How can you be certain of that?" Corrales murmured.

"Because by the time this day is over, Lucifer will belong to me, and I never buy anything except winners."

"Then you are the Jessica Starbuck I have heard so much about!" Corrales exclaimed.

"I'm Jessica Starbuck," she confirmed.

Corrales turned and indicated his two companions. "And these are *mi hermanos,* Lupe and Emiliano."

Lupe Corrales was the fat one, Emiliano the gaunt one. Lupe gave Jessie a surly nod, while Emiliano barely acknowledged the introduction.

Ki cleared his throat and Jessie said, "This is my friend Ki."

Corrales glanced at him, the friendly facade dropping for a moment as he said, "You are Chinese?"

"Japanese," Ki corrected mildly. He had told Jessie once that there was no point in growing angry over the rudeness of a jackass. To do so merely wasted one's time and annoyed the jackass.

Corrales smiled at Jessie again, clearly already forgetting about Ki. "Would you like to watch the race with me, Señorita Starbuck?"

Before Jessie could answer, Don Arturo said, "Señorita Starbuck will be watching the race with *me.*"

"Of course." Corrales put his sombrero on again. "But if you should change your mind, señorita . . ."

13

"I'll let you know," Jessie said coolly.

With a nod, Corrales moved on, taking his retinue with him. As the vaqueros walked past Silencio Ryan, they traded glares with the foreman. Obviously there was no love lost between the crews of the two ranchers.

Hernandez took Jessie's arm and said, "Come with me, my dear. We shall watch the other races before Lucifer demonstrates what a fool Esteban Corrales is for believing that any horse can defeat him."

As Jessie and Don Arturo strolled over to the grandstand, Ki remained behind and looked over the piece of horseflesh they had come this far to buy. Ryan leaned wordlessly on the fence beside him. Ki watched the smooth play of muscles beneath the glossy ebony hide of the horse as it danced nervously around the pen. Even an inexperienced eye could have seen that the long-legged, barrel-chested Lucifer was quite a horse, and Ki's eye was far from inexperienced. He might not have been born a Westerner, but he had lived for many years on the great Circle Star ranch in Texas and knew a good horse when he saw one.

"Skittish, isn't he?" Ki commented after a few minutes.

"Ready to run, I'd call it," Ryan replied.

"That's all right, as long as the horse doesn't tire itself out before the race is even begun."

Ryan laughed. "Lucifer's got more sand than any three other horses I've ever seen. There's not an ounce of quit in him, Ki."

Ki looked over at the man. "You don't talk much like a vaquero."

"Oh, I can cut loose with a string of Mexican cuss words anytime I want to, and riding herd on the crew that I do, that's pretty often. But I grew up speaking both English and Spanish and even a little French. Men from all over the

14

world, other soldiers of fortune my father knew, would visit us when I was a kid. You learn a lot that way. Speaking of which, you talk more like a cowboy than a samurai."

Ki had to smile. Ryan's education in the ways of the world must have been rather extensive; most whites had never even heard of samurai. "I've been both," Ki said quietly.

"I'll just bet you have." Ryan cuffed his J.B. to the back of his head. "That Miss Jessie now . . . she's a thoroughbred if I ever saw one."

"She is the finest person I have ever known," Ki said, a little stiffly.

"I didn't mean any disrespect. I've heard a lot about her daddy, old Alex Starbuck. They say he was a fine man."

Ki nodded slowly, remembering. "Yes. He was."

A cheer went up from the crowded grandstands. Ryan looked in that direction and said, "That'll be the first race. They can't be over any too soon for Lucifer."

Ki turned toward the grandstands. He had no great interest in horse racing, but since Jessie was over there, he ought to be, too, he thought. She was probably safe enough, since she was accompanied by a wealthy, powerful man like Don Arturo, but the attack on them the night before still had Ki wondering.

Had the incident been one of random violence—or was someone here in Monterrey after him and Jessie for some other reason?

Before he could say farewell to Silencio Ryan, something else caught Ki's eye. Some fifty yards away, next to an empty pen, a man was standing and staring toward them. Ki couldn't tell from this distance if the man was looking at him or Ryan or the horse, or perhaps all three. But something about the intense study made a prickle of ice go along the back of Ki's neck.

The man was squat and powerful-looking, wearing the typical clothes of a vaquero and a tall sombrero that shaded his face from the morning sun. A holstered pistol hung from a cartridge belt around his thick waist, and a single bandolier of ammunition crossed his chest.

Ki nudged Ryan with an elbow, nodded toward the watching man, and said, "Who's that?"

Ryan turned and looked. A frown appeared on his face. "Damned if I know. He's watching us mighty close, isn't he?"

"Let's go find out what he wants," Ki suggested. He started toward the watching man, Ryan's long strides matching his own.

Neither of them had gone ten feet, however, when the man wheeled around and vanished into the crowd. Ki stopped and looked puzzled. "I wonder what that was all about?"

"Maybe he's an hombre who appreciates good horseflesh," Ryan suggested. "There's plenty of 'em around."

"Yes, perhaps," Ki agreed distractedly.

But every instinct in his body made him think there was more to it than that. And the attack on him and Jessie the night before was beginning to take on added significance, too. Maybe somebody had heard that Jessie had come here to buy Lucifer, and they might have thought that she had the agreed-upon purchase price of five thousand dollars with her in cash or gold. That wasn't the case, of course; the transaction would be handled by bank draft. But some common thieves wouldn't have known that.

Ki shrugged and turned back toward the pen. "I am going to watch the races," he said to Ryan. "That is, unless you need help with Lucifer . . ."

"We'll be fine," Ryan assured him. "Lucifer won't give

16

me any trouble as long as he gets to stretch his legs pretty soon."

With a casual wave, Ki started toward the grandstand. Along the way, he kept an eye out for the thickset man he had noticed earlier. There was no sign of the gent, though. He could have gone almost anywhere and been swallowed up by the spectators around the racecourse. There were few hiding places better than such a crowd.

Ki climbed into the grandstand and looked for Jessie and Don Arturo. Jessie's blond hair and bright red shirt made her easy to locate. She and Hernandez were sitting in a private box along the front of the grandstand. When she saw Ki coming toward them, she stood up and waved at him.

That was when the gun went off and Jessie fell.

★

Chapter 3

Ki's instincts took over. He shouted, "Jessie!" and threw himself forward toward her. He was vaguely aware of a gun going off again, and this time the bullet made a flat slapping sound as it passed through the air near his head. Then he was at the box where Jessie and Don Arturo had been watching the races. He flung himself down next to Jessie, shielding her body with his own.

"I'm all right, Ki!" she said as she raised herself slightly. "That shot didn't hit me."

"When I saw you fall—"

"Just getting down in case whoever it is kept shooting." Jessie looked over at Hernandez, who was kneeling on the floor of the box nearby. "Are you hurt, Don Arturo?"

The *hacendado* shook his head. "No, the shots missed me as well, señorita."

Still crouched beside Jessie, Ki craned his neck and twisted his head around. There seemed to have been only two shots, but the end of the gunfire hadn't calmed the crowd down any. Some of the spectators were still yelling and screaming in fear, while others either huddled between the benches or pushed frantically toward the exits. Confusion was everywhere.

18

Ki stood up, then bent and grasped Jessie's arm to help her to her feet. "The bushwhacker must have taken off," he said. "If he intended to stir up the crowd, he was successful."

Suddenly more shots rattled through the air, coming from the area where the stalls and pens were located. Don Arturo gasped and exclaimed, "Lucifer!"

Jessie looked at Ki and said, "Come on!" She broke into a run, heading along the aisle of the grandstand toward the exit closest to the pens.

Ki was right behind her, knowing Jessie had probably reached the same conclusion that had leapt into his mind. If someone wanted to steal Lucifer, one way to go about it would be to cause such an uproar that no one was paying any attention to the horse.

If that was the case, then the would-be thieves had not figured on Silencio Ryan. As Jessie and Ki bounded down out of the grandstand and started toward the pens, they both spotted the big redhead crouched behind a water barrel, trading shots with several rough-looking men who were closing in around him. Behind Ryan, on the other side of the fence, Lucifer dashed back and forth, rearing up from time to time to lash out angrily at the air with his hooves. The horse obviously wanted in on this fight.

It would be only a matter of seconds before at least one of the attackers had a clear shot at Ryan. Ki's fingers delved deftly into the pockets of his vest as he shouted, "Hey!"

One of the men spun around to face the new threat, but before he could bring his gun to bear, Ki's hand flicked out with a snap of the wrist. The *bandido* staggered back a couple of steps as one of the razor-sharp *shuriken* buried itself in the soft flesh of his throat. Bright red blood bubbled out over the throwing star, dulling its luster. The man's trigger finger twitched as he died, but the barrel was pointing toward the ground at his feet. The bullet, in fact, blew two of his own toes off, but the man was already beyond feeling any pain. He crumpled to the dirt.

Jessie had veered to one side so that she and Ki wouldn't be bunched together to form an easier target. She had the little derringer in her hand. Another of the would-be thieves whirled toward her, but he didn't get a shot off, either. The derringer cracked wickedly, and the man's right leg went out from under him, the kneecap smashed by Jessie's bullet. He shrieked in pain as he fell, but he held on to his gun and tried to aim it toward her, his hand trembling as he did so.

Jessie was about to fire again when something smacked into her from behind. "Get down, señorita!" a voice shouted, practically in her ear. She fell heavily, with whoever had grabbed her landing on top of her and knocking the breath out of her lungs.

She saw Silencio Ryan fire again from behind the water barrel, saw the head of the man she had just wounded explode as Ryan's bullet caught him in the back of the skull. That left two more men, and Ki had just disarmed one of them with a skillfully thrown *shuriken* that had slashed across the back of the *bandido*'s gun hand. The man clasped his wounded hand and howled in pain, and a second later he flew backward as Ki launched a high kick that caught him in the chest.

Ryan rolled out from behind the barrel and came up in a crouch as the last man broke and tried to run. The redheaded foreman fired twice more, the slugs ripping into the fleeing man and spinning him around a couple of times in a grisly ballet before he flopped onto his face.

Jessie tried to get up, but the man who was lying on top of her held her down. "Be careful, señorita," he said. "Bullets may still fly."

"I don't think so," Jessie said through gritted teeth. "And

I'll thank you to get off me." She was aware that the man's groin was pressed against the soft cushion of her rump more tightly than it needed to be if keeping her safe from flying lead was his only consideration.

"Very well," he said, and a second later the weight came off of her back. She pushed herself onto hands and knees and then stood up. As she brushed some of the dust off her clothes, she looked over and saw Esteban Corrales doing the same thing.

"You're the one who knocked me down, Señor Corrales?"

"But of course. When I saw that man trying to shoot you, my first thought was of your safety."

"Well . . . thank you. But I wasn't really in that much danger."

Nearby, Ki knelt beside the man he had disarmed and then knocked down with a flying kick, and the martial artist's mouth twisted in a grimace of dissatisfaction. Ryan came up, Colt .44 still in his hand, and asked, "How's this one doing?"

"Dead," Ki said curtly. "I miscalculated slightly and broke his neck."

"That accounts for all of them, then. There were only four." Ryan tucked the revolver behind his belt.

"I wanted to take one of them alive so that we could question him."

Ryan frowned. "What is there to question anybody about? They were out to steal Lucifer, no doubt about it."

"Perhaps . . ."

Ki was still wondering, though, if there was any connection between today's violent events and the attack on him and Jessie. He looked at the faces of the dead men, trying to determine if any of them had been the ones who jumped them the night before, on the way to the restaurant. Ki's memory for faces was good.

He decided that he had never seen any of these men before.

Don Arturo came hurrying up, looking worried. Behind him were several men in uniform. "I went to fetch the police," he said. "Is anyone hurt?"

"Only these hombres who tried to steal Lucifer," Ryan replied with a casual wave at the dead men.

Hernandez turned to Jessie. "You are not injured?"

"Only my dignity," she said with a slight smile.

Don Arturo looked at the man standing next to Jessie, and his aristocratic face darkened with anger. "Corrales!" he said. "What are you doing here?"

"I came to the aid of Señorita Starbuck," Corrales answered coolly. "I did not want her to be hurt."

Don Arturo flung a hand toward the corpses. "Perhaps these are *your* men," he accused. "Perhaps you thought to steal Lucifer, so that the race would be called off and no one would know how much faster he is than your El Rey!"

Corrales's mouth tightened. "I had nothing to do with this. I have never seen these men before."

One of the uniformed policemen was studying the faces of the dead men, and as he straightened he said, "I have."

Hernandez turned to the official. "You know who they are, *Capitán* Guzman?"

"I do not know their names, but I believe they are some of the men who ride with Lucardo Perez."

"Perez!" Don Arturo exclaimed. "The bandit? He would not dare send his men right here into Monterrey."

Ki spoke up. "This Perez . . . what does he look like?"

The police captain said, "I have never seen him, but he has been described as a short, powerful-looking man. An ugly man."

"Does he wear a single bandolier?"

The policeman frowned. "So it is said."

22

Ki and Ryan looked at each other. Ryan ran a thumbnail along the line of his jaw, then said, "Perez didn't just send his men to Monterrey, *Capitán*. He came himself. Ki and I saw him just a little while ago, right before the races started."

"Impossible! Not even Perez would dare—"

"The man we saw was short," Ki said, "and he wore a single bandolier."

"Other men could fit that description," Don Arturo pointed out. "But it would be just like Perez to attempt something so daring as to steal Lucifer out of his pen on the day of a race."

"Did anyone see who fired those first shots?" Jessie asked.

The captain shook his head. "No one in the stands was injured. The shots appear to have been a . . . a . . ." He groped for the right word in English.

"Distraction," Jessie supplied, and the policeman smiled and nodded. Jessie went on. "That's what Ki and I thought, too."

The captain glared at the bodies of the dead bandits and said, "I will have some men take this trash away. I suppose today's races will have to be canceled."

"Not at all," Hernandez said sharply. "Señorita Starbuck has come all the way from her ranch in Texas to purchase Lucifer, and she must see him run first. Otherwise how will she know that she is getting what she pays for?"

"Once she has seen the race, she may change her mind and wish to buy El Rey instead," Esteban Corrales said.

"I doubt that," Jessie said. "But if I do . . . ?"

"Ah, then as much as I hate to disappoint a beautiful lady, I would have to do so. El Rey is not for sale."

Don Arturo snorted. "That will not happen, because El Rey has no chance against Lucifer."

"I've heard both of you growling and snapping at each other like two old dogs," Jessie told them. "It's time to put it to the test. Shall we continue with the races?"

Hernandez and Corrales both agreed enthusiastically. Some of the spectators had fled, but most of them were still in the stands, waiting to see what was going to happen. *Capitán* Guzman cupped his hands around his mouth to announce loudly that the danger was over and the races would go on as planned. People were still babbling in a mixture of excitement and fear, but the crowd began to settle down somewhat after Guzman made his announcement.

Don Arturo and Esteban Corrales stalked off, each to his own private box, but Jessie and Ki remained for a few moments at the pen where Lucifer was still moving around skittishly. Jessie asked Ryan, "Exactly what happened when the shooting started?"

The big redhead tugged at his earlobe and frowned in thought. "Well, there were those two shots over at the grandstand, and people started yelling and screaming. I didn't know what was going on, but I thought somebody might be hurt and figured I ought to go check on you and Don Arturo, señorita. I started toward the grandstand myself, but then I happened to glance back and saw those four hombres heading toward Lucifer's pen. Something told me they were up to no good, so I doubled back. The crowd held all of us up, but I got here first. When those bandits saw me, they grabbed iron and started trying to ventilate me. Came too damn close to doing it, too. If I hadn't been able to duck behind that water barrel . . ."

Ki said, "If you hadn't noticed them and come back, they would have gotten Lucifer and led him away in the confusion."

Ryan cast an admiring glance at the big black horse and said, "They would have tried. They might have had more

24

trouble than they expected, though. A stranger would have a hard time taking Lucifer anywhere he didn't want to go."

"What do you know about this Lucardo Perez?" Jessie asked.

Ryan's frown deepened. "He's a bad one, from what I hear. We've never had any trouble with him, since Don Arturo's got the toughest bunch of vaqueros in this part of the country, but he's raided ranches and villages all up and down the Sierra Madre. When he wants something, he doesn't take kindly to anybody standing in his way." Ryan glanced at the horse again. "If Perez has got his sights set on Lucifer, he's not going to be happy about what happened today."

"The happiness of some *bandido* isn't any of our concern," Jessie said. "Anyway, tomorrow Lucifer will be on his way to Texas with Ki and me."

"And me," Ryan added. "I'm not letting that big ol' son out of my sight until we reach Laredo. You'll have some hands waiting there to help you with him?"

"That's right," Jessie nodded. She looked toward the grandstand, where the sound of cheering had grown in recent minutes. The spectators were getting caught up in the thrill of the races again and were forgetting all about the danger and chaos earlier. That was the way it ought to be, Jessie supposed.

Life, like the horse races, went on.

★

Chapter 4

Jessie and Ki returned to the grandstand and sat with Don
Arturo in the rancher's private box while the preliminary
races were run. Despite everything that was on her mind,
Jessie found herself getting interested in the outcome of
the contests. There was something about the pounding of
hooves and the hard, muscular surging of horseflesh that set
fire to the blood. Even though she had no money wagered
on any of these races, she found herself leaning forward
and cheering along with the rest of the crowd.

For his part, Ki sat calmly, his arms folded, a bemused
expression on his face. Despite the years that had passed
since his departure from Japan, this was one North American
custom that was clearly beyond his understanding.

When all the other races were done, Don Arturo sat
forward eagerly on the edge of his seat. "There is Lucifer,"
he said, pointing toward the gate that led onto the racecourse
itself.

Jessie saw Silencio Ryan leading the big black horse onto
the track. A young man who looked to be little more than
a boy was perched on Lucifer's back. "Who's that?" Jessie
asked.

"One of my vaqueros," Hernandez explained. "He is

26

called Tomas, and he always rides Lucifer."

Jessie smiled. "I'm going to hate to take Lucifer away from you. You and Silencio and Tomas are bound to miss him when he's gone."

"*Sí,* this is true, but the reason for my hacienda's existence is to breed fine horses and sell them. Besides, after Lucifer has run his last race and is retired, I expect you to sell me some of the colts he sires, Señorita Starbuck."

"It's a deal," Jessie agreed with a laugh.

A few minutes passed while the crowd waited, its impatience growing. Most of these people were here today to see Lucifer run against El Rey. Finally, Corrales's horse, a leggy roan, was led out onto the course. From this distance, Jessie couldn't see all of El Rey's fine points, but the horse looked like a splendid specimen. He might have looked even better had not Lucifer been right there to overshadow him.

"This should be a good race," Ki said as he watched the horses. "El Rey looks fast."

"He is," Don Arturo admitted. "I would cut off my arm before I would allow Corrales to hear me say such a thing, but his horse is probably the second-best in all of Mexico. Lucifer, of course, is better."

"Of course," Jessie said.

A hush fell over the grandstands as the horses were led to the starting line. Both animals were high-strung and more than ready to race. Their riders had trouble holding them in. When the tension in the air had grown even thicker than the smoke coming from the stacks of the foundries in the distance, the starter finally fired his pistol, sending Lucifer and El Rey lunging forward into full-out gallops.

A great shout came from the throats of the crowd as the horses flew past the first grandstand in a blur of motion. Jessie was aware that her mouth was hanging open, but she couldn't stop herself from gaping. She had never seen even one horse run so fast, let alone two. Lucifer and El Rey were neck and neck at the first turn.

And a gap did not open up between them during their entire first circuit of the track, or during the second. Lucifer edged an inch or so in front on the straightaway, but El Rey made that up on the turns.

All the spectators were on their feet, including Jessie and Don Arturo. Even Ki was standing and watching with intense interest. He leaned over to Jessie and asked over the roar of the crowd, "How many times do they race around the course?"

"Four times," she told him, raising her voice so that he could hear. The horses flashed by before them. "The race is half over!"

So far neither Lucifer nor El Rey seemed to be faltering in the slightest. Jessie took her eyes off them for a moment and looked down the grandstand to the box where Esteban Corrales, along with his brothers Lupe and Emiliano, were watching. Corrales seemed calm, his face almost expressionless, but Jessie sensed that was just a pose. He was as caught up in this race as anyone else. Lupe was shouting and mopping at his damp face with a handkerchief, while even Emiliano seemed excited. Jessie hoped the gaunt man didn't get too worked up; he looked as if too much excitement might kill him.

The horses finished their third circuit of the course, and this time as they ran past the grandstand where Jessie, Ki, and Hernandez watched, the gap between Lucifer and El Rey was slightly bigger. They went into the turn, and once again El Rey tried to make up the difference. This time, however, the long-legged roan was not able to completely close the gap. Lucifer was still a head in front when they reached the far straightaway.

28

As they pounded over the hard-packed dirt, Lucifer drew half a length into the lead. Jessie glanced at Corrales again. He was some thirty feet away, so she couldn't tell for certain, but it appeared that the mask of his features was beginning to show a few cracks. He had to know that El Rey was in trouble.

The horses reached the last turn. El Rey's rider was whipping him savagely with a quirt now, but so far Tomas had barely had to touch Lucifer with his whip. El Rey was unable to make up any ground on this turn, and as they entered the home stretch, Lucifer was three-quarters of a length, then a full length, in the lead. The loudest roar so far went up from the crowd, and Jessie became aware that many of the spectators were shouting Lucifer's name.

The race was over well before the horses reached the finish line. Anyone could see that. El Rey fell almost two full lengths behind, and although he was still running gamely, there was no chance he could catch Lucifer in the short distance remaining. Lucifer was unable to pull away any more, but he still won easily, flashing over the line well in front of his opponent.

Despite his age and his white hair, Don Arturo thrust his clenched fists into the air, howled like a wolf, and capered like a young boy. He pounded Ki on the back and hugged Jessie.

"Magnificent!" he shouted. "Never have I seen such a race! Never!"

Ki looked past Don Arturo and nodded. "Señor Corrales is coming," he said.

Jessie turned to look. Indeed, a grim-faced Esteban Corrales was making his way through the wild crowd toward Don Arturo's box, trailed by his brothers and the vaqueros from his ranch. He managed to stretch his mouth into a pained smile by the time he got there. As he

29

extended his hand, he said, "Congratulations, Don Arturo. Lucifer won, just as you said he would."

"And that fact is like gall in your throat, isn't it, Corrales?" Hernandez crowed. Jessie thought he could have been a bit more gracious about winning, but evidently the rivalry between Don Arturo and Corrales was a bitter one of long standing. She supposed she couldn't blame him for gloating.

"There will be other days and other races," Corrales said, his eyes gone cold and hard. He lowered his hand because it was obvious Don Arturo was not going to shake it. "And besides, there are greater prizes to win." He looked over at Jessie. "Adios, Señorita Starbuck. I hope to see you again."

With that, he turned on his heel and stalked away.

"Ho, ho! Losing is hard for him to take," Don Arturo said.

"I thought he took it well," Ki said. "On the surface, at least. But the look in his eyes was not pleasant."

"No," Jessie agreed. "It wasn't. But there's not much he can do about it now, is there?"

The crowd was leaving now, having seen what they had come to see. Jessie, Ki, and Don Arturo made their way down to the course, where Ryan and Tomas were waiting with Lucifer. Don Arturo greeted his rider with a big, back-slapping hug.

"A wonderful ride, amigo!" the rancher enthused. "You have made everyone proud of you."

Tomas patted Lucifer's sweaty flank. "Lucifer is the one to be proud of. He ran with all his heart."

"Sí," Don Arturo said and nodded. He caught Ryan's hand and wrung it. "You have trained this one well, Silencio."

"Lucifer does the work," Ryan said modestly. "I'd better get him rubbed down and back to the stable."

30

After a few more congratulations, he led the horse away.

"Where are you keeping Lucifer?" Jessie asked.

"There are stables near the railroad station. He is staying there," Hernandez replied.

"Do you have any guards besides Señor Ryan?"

"Silencio is worth any two men—no, any three. He will not allow anything to befall Lucifer. You saw how fiercely he defended him today."

Yes, Jessie thought, but if Ki and she hadn't stepped in, Ryan might be dead now, and Lucardo Perez might have Lucifer. She kept the comment to herself, however, not wanting to throw any cold water on Don Arturo's exuberant mood.

The rancher went on. "Now, I believe we have some business to which we must attend."

"Certainly."

"My carriage will take us to the bank. . . ."

Jessie and Ki went with Don Arturo to his carriage, but on the way Jessie glanced back at the pen where Lucifer was being rubbed down and tended to by Ryan and Tomas.

Tonight, she mused, she might just pay a visit to that stable. After all, by then her business with Hernandez would be concluded, and she would have an investment to protect.

"Who's there?"

Silencio Ryan uncoiled like a cat as he came to his feet. The gun he wore tucked behind his belt came easily into his hand. Jessie admired the way the man moved.

"It's just me, Señor Ryan," she said as she stepped out of the shadows near the door of the stable.

Ryan had been sitting on a stool beside Lucifer's stall, leaning back with the stool tipped up on only two of its legs. His negligent pose had vanished in a twinkling of an eye, however, when he heard the soft scrape of Jessie's booted

31

feet on the dirt floor of the stable. A lantern hung from a peg on the wall, casting a warm yellow circle of light that didn't reach all the way to the outer edges of the stable.

Looking a little sheepish, Ryan put his gun away and said, "Oh, it's only you, señorita."

"Only me? Some women would be disappointed, even insulted, by a comment like that, Señor Ryan."

He rubbed his jaw and grimaced. "Hell, I didn't mean it like that—"

"I know you didn't," Jessie interrupted with a laugh. "You just meant that I wasn't one of Perez's *bandidos*."

Ryan nodded. "That's right. That's exactly what I meant."

Jessie moved over where she could see over the wall of the stall. Lucifer was standing quietly inside, a lot more placid than he had been earlier in the day. "He's calmed down," Jessie said.

"He's always that way after a race. He knows he's done his job, and he's satisfied. He'll get over it pretty soon, though, and then he'll be rip-snorting to do it again."

"Does he mind being touched?"

Ryan shrugged his broad shoulders. "Hard to say. Some folks he takes to, some folks he doesn't. If he doesn't like you, he'll let you know in a hurry. Watch your fingers if you go to pet him. He might try to nip you."

Jessie reached over the wall and stroked Lucifer's shoulder. He turned his head to look at her and blew a breath through his nose, but he didn't shy away or snap at her.

"He doesn't seem to mind when I touch him," Jessie said.

"Well, nobody could blame him for that."

She looked over at Ryan, saw the roguish grin on his face, and said, "Are you alone here tonight, Señor Ryan?"

"For now," he replied. "A couple of the boys will be coming by later to spell me so I can get some sleep before starting north on the train tomorrow. And why don't you call me Silencio, señorita? 'Señor Ryan' sounds too much like my father."

"All right. And I'm Jessie. We're going to be traveling together for a couple of days, so we might as well be friends."

Ryan hesitated for a second, then reached out and rested a hand on her shoulder. "Thought we already were."

Jessie turned, looking up at him in the light from the lantern. "Yes," she said softly. "I think we are."

Ryan leaned forward as she tipped her head back a little. His mouth came down on hers. Jessie's arms went around his neck and drew him closer to her as her lips opened under his. His tongue speared into her mouth and flicked at hers, fighting the eternal duel that had no losers.

Jessie felt her nipples hardening against the silk of her shirt, felt the undeniable warmth and need growing in her belly. She felt, too, the hard urgency of Silencio Ryan's manhood against the softness of her stomach. She brought one hand down and caressed it through his trousers, wanting him to be certain that she desired what was about to happen between them as much as he did.

He cupped her left breast, kneading the globe of flesh through the silky material of her shirt. Jessie moaned deep in her throat. Ryan's fingers found the buttons of the shirt and flicked them open, then spread the garment, baring the creamy mounds tipped with coral peaks as hard as pebbles. When he finally broke the kiss, he brought his mouth to her nipples, closing his lips around first one and then the other as Jessie tangled her fingers in his thick red hair.

Somehow he got her boots and pants off while still driving

her mad with his lips and tongue, and she stood there nude except for the bright red shirt, which was hanging open. Ryan reached hurriedly for his own belt, but Jessie stopped him, murmuring, "Let me." She unfastened the belt and the buttons of his trousers, then slid his trousers down over his hips.

His shaft bobbed free, full and straining, and as Jessie knelt in front of him she lowered her mouth to it, closing her lips around the head. The searing heat of her oral caress made him groan, and his hips would have surged forward, driving him deeper into her mouth, if not for the grip of her surprisingly strong fingers on his hips. She held him there like that, teasing the tip of his manhood with her lips and tongue, until he was breathing as hard and fast as a man who had just run a race.

Jessie thought fleetingly of Lucifer. The comparison was inevitable. Silencio Ryan was certainly hung like a—

"Damn it, come here," he growled, taking hold of her shoulders and lifting her. He had stripped his shirt off, and he pressed her to his bare, fur-matted chest. Tight-lipped, he said, "There's a pile of straw there, but it'd be too damned itchy."

Jessie grinned wantonly at him. "There's bound to be a blanket around here, isn't there?"

Ryan grinned back at her.

Less than a minute later, he was sprawled on his back, atop a blanket spread over the straw, as Jessie straddled him and gripped his shaft lovingly. She lowered herself on it, closing her eyes and sighing as he slid into her channel and filled it completely. She rested her hands on his chest and began rocking her hips back and forth. Her breath hissed between her teeth as her excitement mounted.

Ryan groaned and lifted his hands to her breasts. His fingers tightened on the creamy flesh, molding and caressing.

34

His hips thrust up from the blanket, driving him deeper and deeper into her.

Jessie paced herself, like a rider waiting for the home stretch. Then, as Ryan's manhood swelled even more inside her, she let go of the mental reins and drove for the finish line. The copper-blond mat of fur at the juncture of her thighs ground hard against the thick red forest around his shaft. She cried out as she felt his climax come boiling up the stalk. It gushed into her, filling her with its wet heat. She was drenched by the mixture of their juices.

Then she slumped forward, collapsing on his chest as she gasped for breath. Ryan's arms tightened around her as a final shudder went through both of them.

Jessie wasn't sure how long the train trip from Monterrey to Laredo would take, but she was certain of one thing.

After tonight—after what she had found with Silencio Ryan—it wasn't going to be long enough.

★

Chapter 5

The next morning, Jessie and Ki walked along the platform at the Monterrey train station, then down some steps to the ground. They made their way alongside the train as smoke billowed from the stack of the big locomotive. Their baggage had already been loaded, and seats were waiting for them in one of the passenger cars. But before she and Ki boarded the train, Jessie wanted to make sure Lucifer was loaded safely into the converted freight car in which he would be riding.

As they approached the car, Jessie saw the ramp that had been placed at its door so that the horse could walk up and into the car. Lucifer, however, was not cooperating. The big black stallion was still on the ground, while Silencio Ryan was on the ramp, holding the lines attached to Lucifer's halter and trying to coax his charge up the incline.

"Damn it, you stubborn jughead! Get on up here!" Ryan was saying as Jessie and Ki came up to the car.

"It looks like Lucifer doesn't want to go," Jessie called out to him.

"What?" Ryan snapped, then immediately looked contrite. "Oh, it's you, Jessie—I mean Señorita Starbuck." He took off his hat and sleeved sweat from his forehead. Evidently he had been struggling with Lucifer for quite a while. He went on. "This big fella can be as stubborn as a mule when he wants to be. And I guess this is one of those mornings when he wants to be. Like I told you, he's never ridden on a train before."

"It appears he does not trust you," Ki commented.

"He trusts me, all right. He's just being contrary." Ryan gave the reins another tug. "Come on, Lucifer!"

Jessie climbed up the ramp. "Let me try."

Ryan frowned dubiously and said, "No offense, ma'am, but Lucifer knows me better than he knows anybody else. If he won't cooperate with me, I don't think you'll be able to do any better."

"We'll see." Jessie held out her hand for the reins. "I want to try, anyway."

Ryan shrugged and gave her the reins. Jessie gripped them firmly, took up the slack until the reins were taut, and then said, "Come on, Lucifer. We're going for a ride on this nice train."

The horse jerked his head from side to side and whinnied.

Jessie pulled the reins tight again and said ominously, "Lucifer . . . you're being a bad boy."

The horse blew air loudly through its nose.

"I want you to get into this car right now. It's been fixed up just for you. You have your own stall, and plenty of hay."

Lucifer put one hoof on the ramp.

"That's it," Jessie coaxed. "Just come right on up."

Slowly Lucifer began to walk up the ramp. Silencio Ryan stood in the doorway of the railroad car, shaking his head in wonderment. Jessie kept the reins taut and led the horse past him into the car.

"There," Jessie said. "It's just a matter of knowing how to talk to him."

Lucifer turned his head, looked at Ryan, and curled his lip.

"No," Ryan said, "it's a matter of that mule-headed nag trying to embarrass me, that's what it is."

Jessie laughed and patted Lucifer's shoulder.

Ki came up the ramp and looked around the converted freight car. Two stalls had been built into it, and there was also an area where hay and feed could be stored, as well as a couple of chairs and a cot where whoever was looking after the horse could sleep. The accommodations were spartan, but they would suffice for the two-day journey back to Laredo. Once on the other side of the border, he and Jessie would switch to another train, and this car would be switched as well. Some of the trusted hands from the Circle Star ranch who were waiting in Laredo would assume the responsibility of caring for Lucifer.

"I can stay here with the horse if you would like," Ki offered.

"That's my job until we get to Laredo," Ryan said without hesitation.

"Yes, but I do not mind. You will be on the train if you are needed."

Jessie suspected Ki was trying to arrange things so that she could spend some more time with Silencio Ryan. He probably knew she had gone to the stable the night before, and he likely knew why, too. Somehow, Ki always seemed to know. But he seldom interfered with that part of her life, just as she hardly ever meddled in his personal affairs. For all their years as friends and partners, they each still had things that were private. It was like Ki, though, to try to discreetly pave the way for her.

"Ki can take care of Lucifer, Silencio," she said. "But you do what you think is best."

"Well . . . I reckon we could split the chore," Ryan said.

Ki nodded. "That's the way it'll be, then." He took hold of Lucifer's harness and gently backed the horse into one of the stalls. Just as Lucifer had taken to Jessie right off, he didn't seem to mind Ki touching him, either.

"You two have a way about you," Ryan said as he looked on. "Lucifer's a pretty good judge of character, and he seems to think you can be trusted."

From the doorway of the car, Don Arturo said, "Of course they can be trusted." He came into the car. "I came to say farewell to Lucifer. I hope that is all right."

"Of course it is," Jessie assured him. "As I told you, I hate to take him away from you."

"When he runs his first race for you. I will come to see him," Don Arturo said as he reached over the wall of the stall and patted Lucifer's shoulder.

"And you will be my guest," Jessie said. "In fact, you'll always be welcome on the Circle Star, Don Arturo."

"I accept your kind offer, señorita." The train's whistle blew, shrill and piercing. "Now, however, I must bid you farewell. The train is about to leave."

"And we need to get to our seats."

Ryan said, "I'm going to stay back here until the first water stop, just to make sure the old boy doesn't mind the motion of the train. If everything's all right, Ki can take over then for a while."

"All right," Jessie said. "I don't blame you for wanting to keep an eye on Lucifer for a while, since he's never traveled on a train before."

She patted the horse one last time, then went down the ramp with Ki and Hernandez. The rancher walked with them to the depot platform, where he shook Ki's hand and kissed Jessie's once more. "Adios, my friends," he said. *"Vaya con Dios."*

The conductor called out the order to board, first in

Spanish, then in English. Jessie smiled at Don Arturo and leaned up to kiss him quickly on his weathered cheek. "Good-bye," she said.

A couple of minutes later, the train lurched into motion with the hiss of steam and the clatter of steel. By that time, Jessie and Ki were in their seats, Jessie by the window and Ki beside the aisle. They had berths reserved in the next car, a sleeper, for that night, but they would spend the day here.

The train rolled out of Monterrey, heading north toward home. It would be good to get back to Texas, Jessie thought as she leaned back in her seat and watched the foothills of the Sierra Madre moving past. But between now and then, she intended to spend as much time as she could with Silencio Ryan. She felt warm inside as she remembered their lovemaking of the night before. She looked forward with anticipation to the next time.

Other than that, however, she expected the journey home would be pretty uneventful. . . .

At mid-morning, the train stopped for water in a small village that consisted only of a water tank and a few scattered huts. While the locomotive was taking on water, Jessie and Ki hopped down lithely from the rear steps of the passenger car and walked back to the converted freight car.

Both big sliding doors of the car were open to let air pass through, and Ryan was sitting on one of the chairs. He stood up when he saw Jessie and Ki. He hurried forward to give Jessie a hand as she climbed up into the car. She was wearing jeans, a plain shirt, and her denim jacket, so she was dressed for such things as scrambling into a freight car. Ki climbed in behind her.

"No trouble so far," Ryan reported. "Lucifer's taken to riding on a train better than I thought he would."

Indeed, the big black horse didn't seem any more skittish than usual, Jessie judged. She nodded in satisfaction. "You can ride with me for a while, if you want," she said. "Ki will look after Lucifer."

"Not much looking after to it," Ryan said. "Just make sure he doesn't run out of food or water."

Ki nodded. "Go ahead, Señor Ryan. Lucifer and I will be fine."

"Well, all right. I'll check on you at the next water stop, though."

Ryan dropped down from the car with Jessie and strolled with her back to the passenger car. The long water spout that extended at an angle from the tank to the locomotive was being pulled back into place by the train's crew. The train would be rolling again in a matter of moments.

Jessie and Ryan boarded and settled down in their seats as the train pulled out. For the next couple of hours they sat and talked. Jessie discovered that the wanderlust Ryan had inherited from his father had led him to move around quite a bit as a young man. He had spent time in Texas, Arizona, and California, and had even visited his father's homeland, Ireland, briefly before returning to Mexico to settle down and go to work for Don Arturo. He was a thoroughly charming man, as well as a top hand. An impulse occurred to Jessie, and she mulled it over only a few minutes before saying, "If you ever want to come back to Texas to live, there'll be a job waiting for you on my ranch."

Ryan shook his head without a second's hesitation. "No offense, Jessie, but I'm happy right where I am. My father's gone now, but my mama and her folks all live down here. And Don Arturo's a good man to work for. Besides, I don't reckon I'd be happy knowing that you were my boss. Not after . . ."

"I know," Jessie said quickly. "I should have thought of

41

that myself. But that doesn't stop us from being friends."

"Nope, it sure doesn't."

"And friends are always welcome to visit at the Circle Star."

His hand moved over to rest lightly on hers, and she turned her hand so that her fingers could link with his.

In the afternoon, after they had eaten a lunch of tamales and beans sold by a woman who went up and down the cars hawking her wares from a tray, they went back to the freight car at the next stop and found Ki sitting cross-legged on the floor, rather than on one of the chairs. His eyes were closed and he was breathing deeply.

Ryan frowned. "Is he asleep?" he asked quietly as they climbed into the car.

Jessie shook her head. "Ki is probably more aware of everything that's going on around him right now than we are."

Lucifer stood quietly, staring at Ki as if some sort of silent communication were going on between man and horse. After a moment, Ki opened his eyes and stood up, uncoiling from the floor with a single lithe, efficient motion.

"Everything is fine here," he said.

"I can tell," Jessie said. "Why don't you ride up front for the next stretch, and Silencio and I will stay back here."

Ki nodded and leapt down from the car. He looked back up at them over his shoulder, smiled, and waved.

"Nice fella," Ryan grunted.

"Yes, he is. He's been my best friend ever since I was a little girl." She turned to Ryan and looped her arms around his neck. "But I don't want to talk about Ki right now. In fact, I don't want to talk at all."

She reached up and kissed him.

Ryan's arms went around her, drew her tightly against

42

him. One of his hands slid down her back to the swell of her buttocks, cupping the taut flesh.

The train jerked into motion again a few minutes later. By that time, both Jessie and Ryan were breathing hard, and their fingers fairly flew as they began undressing each other. As the train built up speed, the wind of its passage blew through the open doors of the freight cars and whipped Jessie's thick, lustrous hair around her head. She pushed Ryan's pants down and closed her hand around his erect shaft as it sprang free. It burned like a bar of hot iron against her palm.

"Sit down on the chair," she said breathlessly.

Ryan nodded, putting the back of the chair against the front wall of the freight car to steady it. He sat down, and Jessie knelt, nude, between his knees. She leaned forward and opened her mouth, easing her lips over the head of his erection.

Ryan ground his teeth together, and this time when his hips surged forward involuntarily, Jessie opened her mouth wider and let him drive deeper into her. He buried his fingers in her hair and held her head against him as she swallowed his shaft.

After long, maddening moments, Jessie lifted her lips from him and stood up again, spreading her thighs to straddle him. She was so wet that he slid easily into her as she lowered herself. As his entire length buried itself in her, she put her arms around his neck and held on. The clattering, jerking motion of the train was enough to rock them back and forth. Neither had to move. Ryan kissed her again, then lowered his head so that his lips could leave a burning trail along the soft, curving line of her throat. As he neared the upper slopes of her breasts, Jessie arched her back so that the rosy-tipped mounds lifted and came within easy reach of his mouth, which he applied to both nipples in turn.

"Oh, yes," Jessie moaned as the motion of the train thrust her pelvis against his. "Yes!"

Ryan tore his lips away from her nipples, threw his head back, and let out a hoarse cry as he drove himself deeper into her, so deep that he hit bottom. He held the shaft there, flooding her insides as his climax broke loose.

A second later, so did all hell.

Chapter 6

Ki had let himself doze a little with his black hat tipped down over his face as he leaned back against the seat. The gentle motion of the train was enough to make anybody drowsy. He knew that he didn't have to worry about Jessie, either; Silencio Ryan was with her, and he seemed a good, competent man. Of course, Ki thought with a faint smile, Jessie Starbuck was perfectly capable of taking care of herself. She could probably handle any sort of trouble just as well as anybody on this train, and better than most.

When trouble came, though, it was not what anyone would have expected.

With a wail like a doomed soul, the train's brakes suddenly bit down on the rails. Ki was thrown forward roughly as the drivers reversed. His shoulder struck hard against the back of the seat in front of him. His hat was knocked down over his face, causing him a couple of seconds of intense frustration as he tried to shove it back up where it was supposed to go. Everywhere around him, people were screaming and yelling, and someone was sobbing in pain nearby. The stop had been so abrupt that quite a few people could have been hurt.

In fact, the train had not yet come to a complete halt, Ki realized. It was still skidding forward slowly over the iron rails. With a shudder, though, it finally stopped as Ki came to his feet.

Something was wrong. It didn't take a genius to figure that out.

He had to reach Jessie.

The aisle was already packed with people. Ki looked around desperately, trying to see if there was any other way out. There wasn't. The windows were too small to allow him to climb out through one of them.

Ki glanced up. The ceiling in this car was fairly high. Without pausing to mull it over any longer, he acted on the idea almost instantaneously as it occurred to him.

He stepped up onto the seat where he had been sitting, then put his other foot on the back of the seat. He was closer to the door at the rear of the car than the one at the front, so that was the direction he went. Crouching over so that his head wouldn't hit the polished wood of the ceiling, he started leaping agilely from seat back to seat back, keeping his balance with the skill of a true martial arts master.

The way was fairly clear since most of the passengers had already jammed themselves into the aisle in a frantic attempt to get out of the train. Ki wasn't sure why they had done such a thing without even knowing what was going on. Pure panic, he supposed. If he had not been worried about Jessie, he would have stayed right where he was until it became apparent what had caused the train to stop so violently. Where there were people still in their seats, he hopped nimbly past them, calling out, "Remain still, please!"

Finally he reached the last seat and was about to leap down into the little foyer at the rear of the car. As he poised there, however, a man suddenly appeared in the foyer. He was roughly dressed, wore a high-crowned sombrero, and was brandishing a six-gun.

That was all Ki needed to see. He launched himself off the seat back, his right leg snapping out in a kick as he did so. The heel of his sandal caught the gunman just under the nose, shattering the bones there and driving the shards up and back into the man's brain. The man had time only to grunt in surprise as he fell backward and died, but that was about all.

Ki had been a little off-balance when he started the kick, and the back of a train seat hadn't been the best place to attempt such a move. So he landed badly, coming down in a sprawl on top of the dead man. The upper half of his body was through the open door of the car and onto the small platform at the rear of it. Ki heard a surprised, angry shout from his right and looked that way in time to see another man aiming a pistol at him.

He rolled to the side as the gun blasted, and his cheek was peppered by splinters chewed out of the platform by the bullet slamming into it. The railroad car offered shelter, but he didn't think he could scramble back through the door before the second man triggered again. So he went the other way instead, reaching up to grasp the railing that ran around the platform.

There was another shot as Ki pulled himself up and flipped over the railing, losing his hat in the process. He had no idea where the second bullet went, but he knew he hadn't been hit. He landed jarringly on the ground on the far side of the train and went down on one knee.

The old American saying about the frying pan and the fire flashed through his mind as he looked up and saw three men on horseback spurring toward him. All three of them had guns out and were trying to draw a bead on him as they shouted and yipped. Ki flung himself down and rolled desperately as guns boomed and bullets kicked up puffs of dust around him. He suddenly found himself underneath the

47

train, lying on the rough crossties between the rails.

Well, this was no good, no good at all. The bandits—because that was surely what they were, Ki thought—could simply bend down and shoot underneath the train, riddling him where he lay.

The sides of the passenger car came down slightly lower than the bottom of it, however, and there were all sorts of jutting metal apparatuses along the bottom of the car. Ki reached up and grabbed a couple of struts, hooked his feet over a rod of some sort, and pulled himself up. He flattened himself as much as possible against the bottom of the car. Now if the outlaws wanted to see him, they would have to bend over even farther and peer upward. This might buy him a few seconds of precious time.

But no more than that.

The chair on which Jessie and Silencio Ryan were perched had been wedged against the forward wall of the freight car, so it couldn't go anywhere when the brakes started squealing and gigantic shudders ran through all the cars of the train. The stop was so rough, though, that Jessie and Ryan were still thrown off the chair and to one side. They landed hard, Jessie grunting in pain as splinters from the floor dug into her bare bottom. That might be the least of their problems, though, she thought.

Ryan rolled over onto his stomach, pushed himself up onto his elbows, and shook his head in an attempt to clear it. "What the hell!" he exclaimed.

Jessie ignored the pain in her rump as she scrambled to her feet, grabbed her jeans, and jammed her legs into them. "Get dressed!" she rapped at him. "Something's wrong!"

A second later, as she was reaching for her shirt, she saw what it was. The train trembled to a complete stop, and as it did, men on horseback appeared on both sides of the converted freight car. One of them threw himself out of his saddle and through the open door on that side of the car, howling in glee as he smacked into Jessie and knocked her down. He pawed at her bare breasts as he landed on top of her and laughed raucously.

A second later he was yelling in pain as she raked her fingernails across his eyes and slammed her knee into his groin at the same time. Pushing hard, Jessie shoved him off of her. As she rolled over and started to her feet, she saw more men leaping into the car.

The derringer was behind her belt, but she needed more firepower to deal with this threat. The butt of a holstered revolver was sticking up from the belt of the man she had just momentarily incapacitated. Jessie snagged the gun and jerked it free. She slammed it against the head of its owner, then whirled around, cocking the gun as she brought the barrel up.

The other *bandidos* gaped at her in surprise. Whether it was the sight of the beautiful young blonde wearing only a pair of tight denim pants, or the fact that she was pointing a gun at them and seemed to have every idea in the world what to do with it, either way they hesitated—fatally.

The big revolver bucked against Jessie's palm as she fired, the shots rolling out of the weapon like thunder. Two of the men were driven back as bullets thudded into them. They fell out of the open door on the other side of the car. A third man doubled over and crumpled to the floor, blood welling between his fingers as he clutched at his belly.

Ryan hadn't managed to get his pants on, but he was able to scoop up his gun from the floor. He swung toward Jessie as he eared back the hammer of the .44. "Get down!" he called to her, and she dove to the floor as he fired. A glance over her shoulder showed her the man spinning out of the doorway on that side of the car, blood spurting from his throat where Ryan's bullet had struck him. Ryan leapt to the door, grabbed it, and slammed it shut. He threw the latch to lock it.

By the time he turned around, Jessie had scrambled to her feet and was following his example with the other door. The interior of the car was suddenly plunged into darkness as the door closed with a crash.

"That'll buy us a few minutes," Jessie panted in the darkness.

A second later, with a tiny rasp of noise, she scraped a match from the pocket of her jeans into life. The little flickering glow cast wild, eerie shadows as Lucifer snorted and reared in his stall. The loud explosions and the smell of gunpowder had the horse upset.

Jessie was none too calm herself.

"You'd better get dressed while you've got the chance," she told Ryan. She went over to the stalls and bent to light a lantern that was sitting there on the floor. When she lowered the chimney over the wick, a brighter glare came up and filled the car.

Ryan was already stuffing his legs back into his pants. As he fastened the buttons, he said, "Some gang's holding up the train. Could be Perez's men after Lucifer again."

That had occurred to Jessie as the most likely possibility, too. As she shrugged into her shirt and began buttoning it, she said, "They'll be a little leery of coming in here again, after what happened to the first four men who tried it."

Two of the *bandidos* were still inside the car, both of them unconscious. The gut-shot man had passed out from the shock of his wound and would probably never come to. The man Jessie had hit on the head with his own gun was still out cold. When Ryan was dressed, he took off the man's belt and tied his hands behind his back with it.

They could hear more shots outside, muffled by distance

and the thick doors of the freight car. It sounded as if a full-scale battle were going on. Ryan grimaced and said, "Any suggestions what we do now?"

"We wait," Jessie said as she took bullets from the shell belt of the unconscious bandit and reloaded the gun. She dropped the extra cartridges in the pocket of her shirt.

"Wait?" Ryan repeated.

She took a deep breath, pushed her hair out of her face, and looked up at him. "Ki's out there somewhere," she said. "He'll come to us."

"You sound mighty sure of that."

"I am. As long as he's alive—he'll come."

Chapter 7

They might not find him here, Ki thought, but he couldn't stay where he was and help Jessie, either. He pressed himself flat on the top of the railroad car and tried to figure out what to do next.

He had gotten from the bottom of the car to the top strictly through the intervention of fate. Dumb luck, in other words. Some shooting had broken out farther along the train—from the area of the freight car where Jessie and Ryan and Lucifer were, Ki had thought for one fleeting, frantic moment before regaining control of himself—and the bandits had all ridden off in that direction, whooping and shouting. Maybe they thought one of the shots he'd dodged had finished him off. Ki didn't know or care. All he cared about was dropping back to the roadbed and rolling out from under the car on the side where he couldn't see anybody or even any horses.

There were still *bandidos* on this side of the train, he had observed as he emerged from underneath the car, but they were quite a distance off and none of them were looking in his direction. They were too busy down at the freight car.

The freight car!

Ki forced his mind back into its usual clear, orderly

channels. The ladder leading to the roof of the car was right beside him, and without any more conscious thought, he swarmed up it like a giant spider scuttling up a wall. He transformed from spider to snake when he reached the top, gliding smoothly and soundlessly onto the roof of the car and keeping an extremely low profile as he did so.

Now, as he lay on the sun-heated roof, facing toward the rear of the train, he listened to the gang rampaging through the car underneath him. There were shots and screams, angry yells and pleading wails that were cut off abruptly by more shots. Ki closed his eyes and gritted his teeth for a moment. It was a damned massacre, that's what it was. And there was nothing he could do to stop it. Anything he tried now would only get him killed.

And that would leave Jessie and Ryan to deal with the bandits alone.

Time to get moving again. He came up on hands and knees and crawled rapidly to the end of the car. Raising himself high enough to leap to the next car would be a risk; if any of the *bandidos* happened to be looking up at that moment, they would certainly see him. But the alternative was to lie up here and wait until every innocent on the train, including Jessie, was dead. Ki couldn't do that.

He lifted himself into a crouch and then leaped.

A running start would have been better, he thought as he sailed through the open air over the space between the cars. For a dizzying, terrifying instant, he wasn't sure if he was going to make it. Then his fingers and toes touched the slope at the end of the next car's roof. He found holds where perhaps no other man alive could have and threw himself forward, landing on the flat part of the roof. With all the commotion going on, he thought the noise of his landing had been slight enough to go unnoticed.

He had to make it past this car and another one before he

reached the converted freight car. Sliding along, emulating a snake again, he made it to the next gap between cars and leaped it as he had the first. Again, luck was with him and no one saw him. The shooting and the screaming were dying away now. The bandits were succeeding in taking over the train.

That didn't bode well. When all the other resistance had been crushed, then the outlaws could turn their full attention to the freight car and its valuable contents.

Perez, Ki thought bitterly as he slithered closer to his goal. These bloodthirsty butchers had to be Lucardo Perez's gang. The bandit chief had been frustrated in his attempt to steal Lucifer back in Monterrey, so now he was trying again. And if his men could seize the opportunity to loot an entire train in the process, well, so much the better. It made sense to Ki, and although he knew that Perez's gang wasn't the only bunch of *bandidos* in northern Mexico—not by a long shot—Ki's instincts told him that the squat little thief and murderer was indeed behind this atrocity.

Someday, Ki hoped, he would have a chance to meet Lucardo Perez face-to-face and settle matters with him. Perhaps today, even.

He froze as more shouts came to his ears. The shooting had stopped now. He could catch enough of the Spanish words to know that the gunmen were ordering people off the train. They were making the survivors of the pitched battle get out. But why?

Ki edged closer to the side of the car, just enough so that he could carefully turn his head and peer back up toward the front of the train. He saw a group of people—men, women, and children—huddling off to one side of the railroad tracks. There were quite a few wounded among them, and there was a lot of crying and wailing going on as several *bandidos* covered them with drawn guns. Ki moved quickly back to the center of the roof, fearful that one of the guards would look around and notice him. Listening to the shouted orders, he could tell that the survivors were being ordered out of the other cars. Everyone on the train who could still move was being forced off.

He was beginning to think he knew why, and he didn't like the answer.

Suddenly the whistle blew, and steam billowed from the stack. Ki's eyes widened, and he splayed his arms and legs out even more, searching for all the purchase on the roof that he could find. He heard shouting and the pounding of hooves as some of the bandits mounted their horses again and raced alongside the train. The whistle shrilled once more.

And the train began to move. . . .

Jessie and Silencio Ryan heard the whistle, then were almost jolted off their feet as the train unexpectedly lurched into motion. Ryan put out a hand and caught Jessie's arm to steady her, then stared at her in the lantern light and said, "What in blazes are they doing *now*?"

Jessie swallowed and said, "They must have gotten what they came for."

"The whole damned train?"

She nodded. "The whole damned train."

"That's crazy!" Ryan exclaimed. "Those *bandidos* might hold up the passengers and loot the express car, and if they're Perez's men they've got to be after Lucifer, too. But what the hell are they going to do with a whole train?"

Jessie shrugged. "There's not much we can do now except wait to find out."

Already the train had picked up a considerable amount of speed, but not so much that she and Ryan couldn't have jumped from the door of the freight car and stood a good chance of not breaking anything when they landed. But it stood to reason that some of the *bandidos* might be in the cars behind this one, and if that was the case, they would have no trouble picking off anybody who jumped.

Suddenly another jolt ran through the train, and Jessie and Ryan had to steady each other again. The car rocked dizzingly from side to side.

"It feels like we're turning," Ryan said.

"We are," Jessie agreed.

Ryan shook his head. "This stretch runs straight as a string. I've been over it a dozen times."

"Well, we're turning," Jessie insisted. She made her way to the right-hand door. "I'm going to take a look."

Ryan lifted a hand, acting as if he wanted to stop her, but before he could say anything, she was at the door and had thrown the latch. She shoved the heavy door back on its rollers.

Still rolling past was the same flat, semiarid landscape covered with sparse vegetation that had been outside before. Off in the distance, however, Jessie could make out a dark line running along the ground, and alongside it were strung telegraph poles.

"That's the roadbed!" Ryan practically shouted as he peered past Jessie through the open doorway. "What're we running on?"

He turned and went to the other door, unfastened it, and shoved it open. Jessie looked over her shoulder as Ryan stuck his head out the door.

He yelped and flung himself back in the car a split second later when a bullet smacked into the edge of the door near his head. That sent Lucifer into a fresh round of shrill, angry whinnies. On hands and knees, Ryan moved back toward the center of the car, leaving the door open.

"Some son of a bitch took a shot at me!" he said unnecessarily.

"No one shot at me," Jessie said. "Either they couldn't see the other door from that angle, since the train is still curving around somehow, or they want me alive and don't care about you."

"Thanks," Ryan muttered as he got to his feet and began brushing himself off.

"I didn't mean anything personal by it, Silencio. I'm just trying to figure this out."

He nodded. "Yeah, somebody needs to." He frowned again and ran his thumbnail along his jaw. "I'm starting to remember something. . . . Seems like there was an old spur line that branched off somewhere near here. It ran up into the Sierra Madre, where there were some mines for a while before they played out. But that spur hasn't been used for years. It was in such disrepair trains probably couldn't use it, and I reckon the switch was probably rusted shut."

"Rails can be repaired, and so can switches," Jessie pointed out. "What would the engineer do if he came up on that switch and saw that it had been thrown?"

"Hit the brakes, of course. Especially the way we were barreling along. If that switch was thrown and we'd hit it at that speed, it might've derailed the train."

Jessie nodded. "I'd say there's a very good chance we're on that old spur line, then."

"But who'd go to so much trouble? And *why*?"

Jessie looked into the stall at Lucifer. "A one-of-a-kind horse and some wounded pride . . . those might be good enough reasons for Lucardo Perez."

Ryan slammed a clenched fist into the palm of his other hand. "You're right," he said. "Got to be. Perez and his men are going to take the train up into the mountains, a long way from anywhere, and once they get there they can kill us and steal Lucifer at their leisure."

"Exactly."

"That bastard. To do it, he probably killed a bunch of people."

"From what I've heard, that wouldn't matter to Perez."

Jessie went to the left-hand door and looked out. She could see the mountains, still several miles distant but coming closer as the train angled toward them.

After leaving Monterrey, the railroad followed a route that ran east of the Sierra Madre, through the high, dry near-desert that gradually sloped down to the more fertile coastal plain along the Gulf of Mexico. Eventually the line wound up in Nuevo Laredo, just across the Rio Grande from the Texas town of Laredo.

But this spur line, as Ryan had indicated, ran northwesterly, gradually curving back into the rugged peaks of the Sierra Madre. Jessie had to wonder exactly where the train was bound, and what plans the *bandidos* intended to carry out once they reached their destination, but for the time being, no answers were likely to be forthcoming.

She wondered, too, where Ki was.

He was all right. She had to believe that. If she allowed herself to think otherwise, despair might overwhelm her. But as long as she could cling to the belief that Ki would come for her, she could trust in her own abilities and those of Silencio Ryan and hope that they would all come through this all right somehow.

But if Ki were dead . . .

Furiously Jessie banished that thought from her mind.

The train had picked up more speed and was rocking along at a good clip again, moving somewhat slower than before the *bandidos* had attacked, but not much. Since it didn't appear they would be going anywhere anytime soon,

Jessie decided that she and Ryan might as well put this time to good use.

She unbuttoned her pants, dropped them around her knees, and bent over. "Silencio, can you give me a hand?"

"Uh . . . sure."

"Good. See if you can get some of these splinters out of my butt."

★

Chapter 8

From where he was lying, facing backward, Ki couldn't see the switch coming up, but he felt it when the train jolted past it and began curving toward the west. He looked back over his shoulders at the mountains. Yes, they were definitely coming closer, although slowly because of the angle at which the train was traveling.

It had been a surprise when he realized the train was going to begin moving again; that was the only reason the outlaws would have had for herding all the survivors of the battle out of the cars. But Ki wasn't surprised now that the train had left the main line. If it had gone on north to the next stop, the authorities would have discovered what was going on even sooner.

But by leaving the regular line—and by stranding the passengers back there by the tracks—the *bandidos* had bought themselves some time. Some of the survivors might be able to hike on to the next station, or back to the previous one, but that would take hours. It was also possible that one of them might have the ability to climb a telegraph pole and tie into the line, getting a message through that way. Possible—but not likely. Ki felt fairly certain the bandits would have killed all the train crew outright, except perhaps the engineer if they needed him to run the train. If one of the members of the gang could handle that chore, then the engineer was doubtless dead by now, too.

Ki gave a little shake of his head. He could lie here all day pondering on the plans of the *bandidos,* but only one thing was certain.

Those plans would succeed . . . unless he and Jessie were able to put a stop to them.

It was time to find out if Jessie was even still alive. Stubbornly he refused to believe otherwise, but there *had* been a lot of shooting around the freight car for a few minutes, before the outlaws moved on to the rest of the train.

Ki took a deep breath and lifted his head. The wind caught his long, blue-black hair and blew it around in front of his face. He pulled a rawhide thong from one of the pockets of his vest, gathered his hair, and fastened it at the back of his head. That would keep it out of his eyes.

He slid toward the freight car again, trying to remember what was in the car underneath him. If it was another freight car, he could climb down the ladder at the end, swing himself around to the coupling between cars, and cross it carefully to his destination. If it was a passenger car, however, there would be a door back there, and he wouldn't be able to take the chance of descending. He would have to leap the gap again.

Well, if that were the case, it would be even easier this time than before, he told himself. The motion of the train itself would assist him in crossing the opening between cars. Of course, the landing might be a bit more difficult. If he didn't get a good grip right away, he might be jolted to the side and roll off.

He reached the end of the car and carefully peered down. Damn! It was a passenger car, and it was entirely possible that some of the members of the gang were riding in it. He couldn't risk climbing down.

Ki gathered himself, ready to rise and make the leap to the freight car. He lifted himself to his hands and knees and was about to push off when, over the rumble of the locomotive and the clattering of the wheels on steel rails, he heard an angry shout behind him.

Ki's head jerked around. He saw a man in a sombrero and crossed bandoliers climbing on top of the car from the ladder at the front end. The *bandido* wore two pistols, and he grabbed at one of them while steadying himself with his other hand.

Ki's hand darted into one of the pockets of his vest and came out with a *shuriken.* Letting his instincts take over, he threw it with a sharp flick of his wrist. It was asking a lot to make an accurate throw over such a distance, though— the entire length of the railroad car—and to his dismay, Ki saw the sharp-pointed throwing star sail past its target harmlessly. The bandit must have seen the sun reflecting off the *shuriken,* however, because he flinched as he pulled the trigger of his revolver.

The gun blasted, and the slug smacked into the roof of the car, less than a foot away from Ki, before glancing off. Ki rolled to the side, reaching for another *shuriken* as he did so. The *bandido* fired again, and this time the bullet tugged at Ki's vest. As he started to slide, he had to drop the *shuriken* he had plucked from his pocket and grab for a better hold.

There was none to be had. The roof of the car was crowned, and it was flat only in the very center. When he had instinctively rolled away from the bullets, Ki had put himself at even more risk. Now he was sliding toward the brink with no way of stopping himself.

His feet went over the edge first, kicking at empty air.

Then his legs passed over the small ridge at the edge of the car's roof. Ki's hands slapped one last time at the smooth surface of the roof, trying to slow his descent. Then there was nothing but air underneath him and he plummeted off the side of the car.

Except for his fingers, which found the ridge, less than an inch high, and locked on to it like iron. Gravity pulled his body down, slamming it into the side of the car, but he managed somehow to maintain his grip. Excruciating pain shot from his hands down through his arms and into his shoulders as his weight was supported only by the tenuous hold of his fingers.

Then one of his scrambling feet found the sill of a window in the car, and his fingers sang in relief as he was able to take some of the weight off them.

The next instant, the glass in the window shattered as someone inside the car fired a bullet through it.

The bullet burned a fiery path along Ki's right side, just below his ribs, but he thought it was only a crease, nothing serious. The next shot was likely to be more accurate, though. He could hear the *bandidos* shouting inside the car.

Ki couldn't stay where he was; he knew that. Nor could he go down. That left only one direction.

Up.

And as he lifted his head, he saw the *bandido* who had climbed atop the car grinning down at him, one arm extended out to the side for balance while he aimed his pistol with the other hand. The yawning black muzzle of the gun was pointed at Ki's head.

Ki took the weight of his body on his tortured fingers again as he kicked up with his right leg. His foot caught the ridge at the edge of the car's roof, and every muscle in his body bunched and strained as he pulled himself up literally by his fingers and toes. He heard the gunman on top of the car fire again, felt the kiss of the bullet as it whispered past his cheek. Then he crashed into the bandit's legs.

The man screamed as he toppled over Ki and off the train. That scream was cut off by a crunch as the *bandido* slammed headfirst into the rough ground alongside the tracks of the spur line. The man sprawled there, still and lifeless, and was left behind as the train rolled on.

Ki dug in his toes against the ridge and gradually worked his way around until he was lying perpendicular to the edge of the car, facing toward its center. He was on his belly and had his arms spraddled out, the fingers and palms of his hands pressing down hard on the roof. Now that he wasn't sliding, he could hold himself here like this.

But that wouldn't do him any good in the long run. Taking a deep breath, he began working his way inch by inch up the slope toward the flat area at the center of the roof.

More shouts came to his ears. The men inside the car must have seen their *compadre* go sailing off the edge to his death, because two more of them were climbing on top of the car at the front end. Ki had just reached the center of the roof and was lying there with his muscles trembling from the strain when he saw them coming toward him, guns drawn.

This time when he came up on his knees, he used one of his little throwing knives, rather than a *shuriken*. It was heavier and would travel truer—he hoped. The *bandido* in the lead fired, the bullet going wide past Ki, and the next instant, steel flashed through the afternoon sunshine before burying itself in the man's belly. He cried out, pawed at the hilt of the knife, and then tumbled to the side, landing on his shoulder and rolling over a couple of times before he shot off the side of the car.

That left the second man, and Ki was ready for him. Reaching deep inside himself for every reserve of strength and stamina that he possessed, Ki surged to his feet and launched himself into a kick. Both feet snapped out and drove into the midsection of the remaining bandit. The man was knocked backward.

Ki fell, too, but he landed properly and regained his feet in an instant, in time to see the bandit's gun go sliding off the side of the train. The man had dropped the weapon when he fell, but he had managed to stay in the center of the roof, too, and was even now climbing back onto his feet, his ugly, beard-stubbled face twisted in a grimace of rage and hate. He reached behind his back.

The sun gleamed on the long, heavy blade of the machete the man jerked from its sheath. With a shout, he threw himself toward Ki and slashed out with the machete.

A pounding even louder than the noise of the train was hammering inside Ki's head. He knew it was his pulse. He was almost at the end of his rope, his strength gone, all his inner resources exhausted. Even as he ducked under the machete, he could feel himself slowing down. He dodged again as the man backhanded the blade at his head.

Sooner or later, one of those swipes was going to connect, Ki knew. When it did, his head would leap off his shoulders, bounce off the train, and go rolling along beside the tracks like some sort of grisly child's toy.

Ki couldn't accept that fate. He let the machete pass over his head once more as he ducked, then he threw himself forward at the *bandido,* butting his head into the man's stomach. Both of them fell.

Ki's hand shot up as he landed on top of the *bandido*. The heel of his hand slammed into the man's chin, making his head snap back against the roof of the car. The double impact was enough to knock the man senseless. Ki plucked the machete from the bandit's suddenly loose grip and stood up. A hard shove with his foot sent the unconscious man sliding off the side of the car. Ki stood there holding the machete and watching as the bandit's body disappeared.

Something smacked through the roof at his feet and whistled ominously past his ear.

More bullets slammed through the roof and whined around him. The *bandidos* inside the car must have been watching through the windows, and as soon as they had seen both of their men fall off the car, they knew that Ki was alone up there once more. Not wanting to lose anyone else, they were pouring a fusillade of lead through the roof.

Ki knew he had to move fast. He spun around and ran lightly toward the rear of the car, not worrying now about being careful. If he stayed in one place an instant too long, slugs would tear through him. As he ran, more bullets chewed through the wood right behind his feet.

The gap between cars was coming up quickly. Ki readied himself to make the leap. As he launched out into space, something slapped hard into his left hip. He cried out.

The bullet had only clipped him, but the impact was enough to throw him off balance. Instead of landing catlike on his feet, he sprawled awkwardly on top of the freight car. The only thing that saved him was that the roof of this car was flat all the way across, rather than crowned like the roof of the passenger car. He rolled over and came up onto his knees, shaking his head. He discovered he still held the machete in his hand. Quickly, he scuttled toward the edge of the car.

After everything he had gone through to get this far, it would be simplicity itself for him to grasp the edge of the roof and swing down through the open door of the freight car. Then he would discover if Jessie and Silencio Ryan were still inside with Lucifer and unharmed. He slid the machete behind the belt at his waist and tried to ignore the burning pain in his hip as he reached the edge of the roof and let his legs slide over it.

He dropped, his weight hitting his protesting fingers once more, and hung there for an instant in front of the open door. In that frozen moment of time, he saw Jessie and Ryan, both staring wide-eyed at him, evidently unhurt.

Then, from the next car, a rifle cracked wickedly, and a bullet bored a white-hot path through the meat of Ki's right forearm.

He cried out in pain and frustration as his grasp weakened. His left hand and arm, already badly abused, could not support his weight. His fingers slipped from the edge of the roof, and he felt himself falling.

"Ki!" Jessie screamed.

His toes hit the floor at the very edge of the door, and for a split second he thought he was going to tumble into the car, rather than out of it. But his weight was going backward, and although Ryan lunged at him, trying to get hold of his vest, the big redhead's fingers only barely brushed the front of the garment. Ki's toes slipped and he fell back, finally out of all contact with the train. The freight car whipped past him, carrying Jessie and Ryan out of sight.

Ki slammed into something, bounced off, fell some more. He wasn't sure how that was possible, but there was no time to think about it. He couldn't have pondered on the question anyway, since his brain had finally gone as numb as the rest of him. He fell, crashed into something, and fell again, rolling over and over as he bounded down a steep slope. With each impact, the darkness and the numbness closed in even more around him, until, when he finally came to a stop, he didn't even know it.

He had gone somewhere far, far away, and he heard birds

singing and the delicate music of wind chimes hanging in the trees and smelled the sweet perfume of flowers, and suddenly he was back in Japan and he smiled somehow as unconsciousness completely claimed him.

Chapter 9

Jessie had been bent over as Ryan used his pocketknife to gently pry the last of the splinters out of the smooth, creamy flesh of her rump, when they heard the shots coming from the next car up ahead in the train. Despite the pain of the splinter removal, Jessie had been halfway enjoying the process, especially when Ryan leaned forward to kiss each spot where he took out a splinter.

But when the shooting started, she quickly pulled up her pants and fastened them again, turning to Ryan to say, "Somebody's putting up a fight. I guess the *bandidos* didn't get everybody cleared out of the train after all."

"You think it's Ki?" Ryan had asked.

"There's a better chance of that than anything else."

And indeed, after a few tense moments of waiting, during which the shooting stopped and then started again, much more furiously than before, there had been a loud thump on top of the car. A moment later, Ki's familiar figure had appeared in the doorway as he swung down from the roof. Jessie's heart leapt at the sight of him.

Then, in the flickering of an eye, everything had changed.

Someone in the car ahead must have leaned out a window with a rifle and scored a lucky shot, because Jessie heard the spiteful crack and saw blood spurt from Ki's arm. Ryan lunged at him, trying to grab him and pull him in, but it was too late. Ki fell back, vanishing as he plummeted away from the train.

Jessie screamed.

She was still shuddering and crying now, a couple of minutes later, as Ryan held her in his arms and she buried her face against his broad chest. Awkwardly, he patted her on the back and said, "It's all right, Jessie. I won't let anything happen to you. It's all right."

"No, it's not!" she cried wretchedly. "Ki's gone! He—"

Abruptly she broke off her complaint and took a deep, shuddering breath. Ki might be gone, but the influence he had exerted on her for many years was still with her. She lifted a hand and used the back of it to wipe away the tears that welled from her eyes. From Ki, and from her father, too, she had learned the value of never giving up. She would honor the memory of both men by refusing to let despair overwhelm her. She would continue to fight against whoever was responsible for this outrage.

Besides, Ki might not be dead. True, he had been shot and had fallen from a speeding train, but she had seen him survive many other times when any normal man would have been dead a dozen times over.

"We'd better take stock of the situation," she said. "We've got three revolvers and plenty of ammunition, plus my derringer. That's quite a bit of firepower."

"Yes, but from all the shooting we heard, there may well be twenty or thirty of those bandits on the train, maybe more," Ryan pointed out. "Three guns against that many men doesn't amount to much."

"True enough," Jessie mused as she glanced toward the stall where Lucifer still moved around skittishly, "but we've got a secret weapon."

"The horse?" Ryan sounded dubious. "Lucifer's smart as

all get out, but even so he can't fire a gun."

"No, but what *can* he do better than anyone else?"

The light dawned on Ryan's face. He said fervently, "That horse can *run*."

"Exactly. And when the train finally stops, that's just what he's going to do." Jessie glanced out the door of the car. The mountains of the Sierra Madre were much closer now, and drawing closer all the time. "Let's lead him out of that stall and get him saddled. We want to be ready whenever this train gets to where it's going."

It was a desperate plan, there was no denying that. But as far as Jessie could see, it was their only chance. As soon as the train came to a stop, in the few seconds it would take for the *bandidos* to disembark, she and Ryan would leap from the freight car, mounted on Lucifer, and take off hell-bent for leather. Lucifer was well rested, and even carrying double, Jessie was willing to bet that the big black stallion could cover ground in a hurry. She didn't think that the bandits would start shooting at them—after all, if Perez was responsible for this raid, then capturing Lucifer was likely his primary objective—and Jessie was confident that Lucifer could outrun any pursuit on horseback.

Of course, if she and Ryan got away, then they would be on their own in the middle of the Mexican wilderness with only a little water and no food, but she would trade that for being captives of Perez any day.

Ryan had the saddle on Lucifer. As he tightened the cinches, Jessie said, "When the train stops, you'll be in the saddle. I'll ride behind you."

"That'll put you in the greatest danger," Ryan protested. "You ought to ride in front, so I'd be between you and Perez's men."

Jessie shook her head. "They've already demonstrated

that they're reluctant to shoot at me, but they don't mind taking potshots at you."

"We don't know that for sure," Ryan said with a frown. "Maybe they just saw me and didn't see you."

"Well, whatever," Jessie said with a shrug. "The important thing is that Lucifer is accustomed to you and you're accustomed to him. You can get the most speed out of him. And while you're doing that, I'll use a couple of these revolvers and make things as hot as possible for the bandits. If they're busy ducking lead, they can't be throwing it at us nearly as accurately."

"I reckon you're right," Ryan agreed grudgingly. With the toe of his boot, he prodded the bandit who was still alive. The man had regained consciousness a little earlier, and he scowled murderously up at Ryan. "What'll we do with this one?" Ryan asked Jessie.

"Leave him here tied up, I suppose."

"You sure we can't cut his throat before we bust out of here?"

Jessie thought about Ki, and for a second the idea of killing the *bandido* held an undeniable appeal for her. But she wasn't a cold-blooded murderer, no matter what. She shook her head.

"Cutting his throat sounds good," she said, "but the smell of all that fresh blood might spook Lucifer even more. We don't want that."

The bandit swallowed hard as he looked at her. He probably thought his life was hanging by a more slender thread than it really was, but that was all right with Jessie. Let the bastard stew awhile, she told herself.

Without venturing too close to the door, Ryan looked out at the mountains. "We're getting close," he said. "You can tell the grade is a little uphill now. We're entering the foothills."

"How far into the mountains were those mines you mentioned?" Jessie asked.

Ryan shook his head. "Don't know for sure. I was never up there. I don't know how far this spur line extends. But I'd say we ought to be there in an hour or less."

Jessie looked grimly at the mountains. "Can't be too soon for me," she said.

Silencio Ryan's prediction proved to be accurate. Jessie estimated only a few minutes more than an hour had passed when she heard the squeal of the brakes and felt the train beginning to slow down.

The surrounding countryside was even more rugged now. Boulder-strewn hills thrust up all around, and steep-sided canyons cut through them. Looming even higher were the mountains themselves, the peaks somewhat rounded by the passage of thousands of years, but still gray and foreboding. The train slowed even more, and from the doorway Jessie spotted several old mining shafts sunk into the hillsides, with ancient tailings spread out in fan shapes beneath the openings, which reminded her somehow of dark, yawning mouths. She saw, as well, occasional piles of rubble that were all that was left of the cabins where the miners had lived. They had taken silver and gold out of these hills until all the veins had run dry, and now all that was left were the ugly reminders of the past.

Ryan swung into the saddle as the train shuddered and slowed even more. "Better mount up," he said to Jessie.

She turned away from the doorway. She had taken the gunbelts from both of the *bandidos* in the car and strapped them around her waist, after using Ryan's knife to make new holes in the leather so that the buckles would fasten. Holstered Colts rode on both of her hips, the one on the left resting butt-forward since she'd had to wear the shell belt backward. She slipped her denim jacket on and then reached up to take the hand Ryan extended to her. She used the stirrup to give herself a boost and slung her right leg over Lucifer's back as she stepped up.

"You hold on tight when we come out of this car," Ryan cautioned her. "It won't do us any good if you go sliding off when we land."

"Don't worry about me," Jessie told him. "Just get this horse running as fast as he can, as quick as you can."

"Any idea where we ought to head?"

"Anyplace where the ground is fairly level and Lucifer will have a chance to outrun the pursuit. You probably ought to head up one of these canyons that keep branching off."

Ryan nodded. The train was almost at a standstill now, just barely creeping along. "Hang on," he warned. "We're getting the hell out of here!"

Jessie tightened her arms around Ryan's waist and pressed herself to him so that her breasts flattened against his back as he dug his heels into the flanks of the big black horse. Lucifer hesitated only an instant before plunging out through the open doorway of the freight car. Behind them, the tied-up bandit screamed lurid curses in Spanish as they left the car.

For a dizzying couple of seconds, Jessie and Ryan were airborne atop Lucifer, then the horse's forehooves hit the ground with the clarion ring of steel against stone. Jessie heard shouts of alarm and twisted her head to look toward the engine. Several of the *bandidos* came pouring off the train, and they were yelling and pointing at the fugitives.

Lucifer stumbled a bit when he hit the ground running, but within seconds he had settled down into a strong, steady gait. Jessie reached down with her right hand and closed her fingers around the smooth wooden grips of the revolver holstered on that hip. As she slid it free and eared back

74

the hammer, she called to Ryan, "Get ready for some loud noises!"

"Pretend it's the Fourth of July and set off some fireworks!" he shouted back.

She twisted just enough on Lucifer's back to reach across with the pistol and bring it to bear on the startled outlaws. Ryan flinched a little, involuntarily, as the weapon began to crash right behind him. Jessie triggered off three shots and had the satisfaction of seeing the *bandidos* leap frantically for cover as the slugs kicked up dust around their feet.

Jessie looked the other way, and sure enough, there were bandits in that direction, too. She brought the gun around, glad that she had loaded the sixth chamber in the cylinder instead of letting the hammer rest on an empty, as was normally her habit. She emptied the revolver at the second bunch of cutthroats.

By now Lucifer had covered several yards and was building up even more speed. Ryan had his nose pointed at one of the nearby canyons. If they could reach the canyon, Jessie thought, they stood a good chance of getting away, because they would have a good lead by the time they got there. And the way the canyons twisted and turned crazily in this rugged terrain, it was likely she and Ryan could give Perez's men the slip.

Unless, of course, the canyon they chose was a dead end. If that were the case, the term "dead end" might apply in more ways than one.

Jessie holstered the right-hand gun and drew the one on her left, twisting her wrist to grasp the forward-facing butt of the revolver as she did so. She looked over her shoulder again. The *bandidos* had opened the doors of one of the other freight cars, and they were jumping their horses out through the opening. Within a matter of minutes, Jessie knew, they would be pursuing the escaping prisoners on those mounts.

But a matter of minutes might as well have been a lifetime, she thought, because with every second that ticked by, Lucifer put more distance between them and their erstwhile captors. With a big lead, there wasn't a horse short of the Rio Grande that could catch the magnificent black stallion.

Jessie threw a couple more shots at the train, just to remind the *bandidos* that she and Ryan were armed and didn't mind using their guns. As she had expected, the bandits had not tried to shoot them out of the saddle or to down Lucifer with gunfire. Either the horse—or her— or both of them—were too important to the outlaws to risk their lives.

Ryan looked back, too, and let out a whoop of triumph. "We're going to make it!" he shouted. "None of those nags are ever going to catch Lucifer!"

The entrance to the canyon was close now. Several large boulders closed off part of it, but Ryan would be able to swing the surefooted Lucifer around them without even slowing down much. He tugged carefully on the reins to do just that; Lucifer responded better to a light touch than to a rough one.

Without breaking stride, Lucifer slowed down slightly and galloped around the boulders, passing from the bright sunshine of late afternoon into the shadows cast by the tall walls of the canyon. Jessie blinked as her eyes tried to adjust. She saw something in front of them and let out a warning shout.

Ryan saw the obstacle, too, a pile of dead brush that had been dragged into the center of the trail. There was only one thing to do, and Ryan did it instantly. Since the way ahead was blocked, and since they couldn't turn back or even veer to the side because of the rocks, the big redhead hauled back on Lucifer's reins and shouted urgently, "Up, boy! Take it!"

Lucifer had not been trained as a jumper, but instinct and loyalty to Silencio Ryan told the horse what to do. He obeyed the command, his hind legs bunching as they drove him up and over the makeshift barrier. His hooves barely tipped the brush as he soared over it.

They would have made it if that was all there had been to it. The canyon floor ahead was flat and clear. But as Lucifer landed, against stumbling just the slightest bit, lassos came sailing out from the rocks clustered next to the walls of the narrow canyon. They were reatas, the long, incredibly strong ropes made of braided rawhide and preferred by Mexican vaqueros. Whoever had cast these loops were experts at it, because both of the ropes settled over the shoulders of Jessie and Ryan.

Jessie cried out as she realized what was happening, in the split second before the loops tightened. The reatas snapped taut, and both she and Ryan were jerked unceremoniously from the back of the racing stallion. Lucifer galloped on as his riders were dumped painfully on the hard-packed dirt of the canyon floor.

The impact knocked the breath out of Jessie. She gasped and moaned and struggled futilely against the rope. Beside her, Ryan was not moving, and she hoped that he had only been knocked senseless by the fall. Such a mishap could have broken his neck.

She heard footsteps approaching and stopped struggling. There was no longer any point to it. She and Ryan were caught, good and proper. A moment later, several men on horseback dashed past them, heading up the canyon after Lucifer. Without a rider to direct him, they would probably be able to catch up to him and lasso him, at least eventually.

The men who were on foot came up to Jessie and Ryan. She could see their booted feet now, and the boots looked more expensive and well cared for than she would have expected from a bunch of bandits. Their trousers were brown whipcord with golden threads filigreed up the sides in ornate patterns.

A smooth voice said, "How nice of you and Señor Ryan to meet us halfway like this, Señorita Starbuck. I thought we would have to go all the way down to the train to fetch the two of you."

Jessie looked up in amazement. Instead of the ugly, beard-stubbled features of Lucardo Perez, which she had expected to see leering down at her, she was staring at the handsome, clean-shaven face of Esteban Corrales.

★

Chapter 10

If this was truly death, then it was not so bad, Ki found himself thinking. Everything was pitch-black, to be sure, but there was a pleasant smell in the air and something smooth and cool was stroking itself across his forehead.

Perhaps it was dark only because his eyes were closed, and if he opened them, he might find himself in the afterlife, which he pictured as a beautiful garden filled with flowers and trees and lovely geishas who would attend his every need and satisfy his every whim. Yes, he decided, he should at least *try* to open his eyes.

Before he could summon up the strength to do so, the cool, smooth thing on his forehead went away, and he heard a strange rasping sound near his ear, as if something were being dragged across a sandy surface. Without even thinking about it, he shifted his body and rolled onto his side, and a moan burst from his mouth as pain exploded in every part of his being.

Over the sound of the moan, he heard something else— a low, rattling buzz. The noise was unmistakable.

Ki's eyes flew open, his nerves galvanized by that familiar sound, and he found himself staring at a huge, coiled rattlesnake some twelve inches from his face.

He froze, fighting down the instinct that boiled through his blood and told him to jump up and yell. If he tried to do that, the snake would surely strike him, probably in the face. His death would be fairly rapid but still hideous, and now that he had realized he was alive, he wanted to stay that way.

Breathing shallowly, Ki tried to figure a way out of this dilemma. Snakes relied primarily on their sense of smell, he knew, although they could see and hear well enough to recognize a threat, especially at a short distance like this. This rattler was definitely in a defensive posture, coiled tightly, with its tail lifted and the rattle at the end of it whirring furiously, whipping back and forth so rapidly that it was only a blur.

Somehow Ki had to get the snake to calm down.

He realized now that the sensation he had felt on his forehead a few minutes earlier had been the snake's belly as it glided across him. At that time, it had not regarded him as a danger. Perhaps if he could remain perfectly still for long enough, the snake would lose interest in him and slither away. As far as Ki could tell, that was his only real chance to get out of this alive.

Ki slowed his breathing even more. He could, when called upon to do so, reduce the rate of his breathing until it appeared to all but the keenest observer that he was dead. He had to do that now, and the judge he had to fool was the huge diamondback rattler. He could feel his pulse slowing as he concentrated intensely on what he was doing.

Seconds crept by at an excruciatingly slow pace. The buzzing was quieter now, however, and when Ki looked at the snake's rattle, he could see that it had slowed down. He could make out the segmented appendage itself, instead of just the blur it had been a few minutes earlier. This was going to work, Ki sensed. If he could just hold out for a few minutes longer, the snake would give up and crawl off, and then he could move again.

Gradually, the snake's tail stopped rattling and lowered. The snake watched Ki for several moments longer, its cold black eyes implacable as stone and as evil as the marble of an ancient altar where the hearts of living virgins were hacked out and lifted high and blood-dripping over the heads of cackling priests. Ki suppressed a shudder as that thought went through his brain. The snake began to uncoil, the loops of its body sliding over one another.

Then some damned fool yelled, "Do not move, señor!"

Instantly the rattler coiled again, its head raised and swaying back to strike. Ki's eyes widened in horror, but there was no time to get away from the creature. It darted forward, mouth wide and fangs poised—

The snake's head exploded in a welter of blood as a gun blasted somewhere above Ki. Momentum carried the snake forward so that the gruesome ruin where its head had been an instant earlier slapped across Ki's face. He shouted, the sound welling up his throat uncontrollably, and flung himself away in revulsion to lie facedown and shuddering a couple of feet from where he had been. Agony smashed through his skull with every beat of his heart.

Dirt and gravel pattered down around him, striking him lightly on the back of his head and his shoulders. He forced himself to lift his head and see what was happening now. Blinking his eyes against the grit that floated into them, he focused on a figure sliding down a steep, rocky slope toward him. The shape was silhouetted against the sky overhead so that Ki could not make out any details, but it was carrying something that was probably a rifle. A smaller shape came down after it.

A moment later, sandaled feet struck the ground close beside Ki. Strong hands gripped his shoulders and rolled him over onto his back. The shape loomed over him, moving between his eyes and the sun. Ki blinked again, grateful for the shade.

"Good Lord, you're a Chinaman!" a man's voice exclaimed in English.

That fact barely registered on Ki's brain. His throat worked for a moment, and sound rasped hoarsely from it, the words making their way past dry, cracked lips.

"J-Japanese . . . and American . . ." he croaked.

"Well, whatever," the man said. "I knew you were some sort of Celestial. Didn't know if you were alive, though, before I squeezed off that shot. You were lying so still with that rattler curled up beside your head, I thought you might already be dead."

"Close . . ." Ki breathed. "Too close . . ."

"Amen to that. Here, let me lift your head. Ana, give me that canteen."

The man got a large, knobby hand underneath Ki's head and supported it while he held a canteen to Ki's mouth with his other hand. The water was warm and rather alkaline, but to Ki it tasted like pure ambrosia. He took a healthy swallow and would have gulped down more had the man not taken the canteen away.

"That's enough for now, until we find out just how bad you're hurt. Can you sit up?"

"I can try," Ki said.

"Good. I'll give you a hand. Ana, get that snake's carcass out of here before it starts to draw flies."

The man slid an arm around Ki's shoulders and lifted him even more. Ki's vision spun crazily as he pushed himself into a sitting position. He groaned and lifted his hands to his head. His right arm was stiff and painful, sending fresh twinges of pain through him every time he moved it.

"Got a bullet hole in that wing, don't you?" the man

asked. "Well, I won't ask how it got there, not yet. You can explain all that later, along with how come you got thrown off a train."

"How . . . how did you know?"

"You're at the bottom of a dry wash that has a trestle over it, up yonder about fifty feet. I can see the marks all the way down the side of the arroyo where you bounced off it. That probably saved your life if the train was going as fast as it appears to have been. You were able to expend your momentum by sliding down the slope. If you'd landed on flat ground, the impact would have likely broken every bone in your body and caused substantial internal injuries. Of course, you may have some of those anyway. I can't tell yet and won't be able to until I get you back to my place."

Whoever this stranger was, Ki thought, he was damned talkative. But that was all right. Ki owed the man a debt that probably could not be repaid. While it was true that the man's shout had goaded the rattlesnake into striking—after Ki had lulled the reptile into leaving him alone—the snake was not the only danger Ki faced out here. Even if the snake had slithered off, Ki, alone and hurt in the middle of nowhere, would still have been in bad shape.

Now he had someone to help him, and the man was still talking. "What I can't figure out," the stranger went on, "is what a train was doing on that old spur line in the first place. It hasn't been used in all the time I've been down here, and that's going on five years."

"The story is . . . too long . . . to tell now," Ki said.

"I expect you're right about that." The man stood up and bent over, looping an arm around Ki's midsection. "Come on, let's get you on your feet."

Ki felt another moment of extreme dizziness as he was lifted, then his head began to settle down a little. He looked up and saw that the man had been telling the truth; the marks of his violent descent were visible on the side of the arroyo, and up above was the trestle where the spur line crossed over the dry wash. When he had been shot off the train, he never noticed where he was about to land. Pure luck had sent him tumbling down here.

For the first time, Ki took a good look at his rescuers. The man was several inches taller than him but probably weighed less; the clothes he wore hung loosely on his slender frame. The garments were peasant garb, from the sandals on the man's feet to the wide-brimmed straw sombrero on his head. The man's face was long and lean, like the rest of him, and he had a lantern jaw and deep-set eyes. His skin was burned and weathered to the point that Ki would not have guessed that he was a white man except for his voice. It still held a trace of an Eastern accent.

There was a young woman with the man. He had called her Ana, Ki remembered. She was no more than twenty, he judged, perhaps less. He based that on her quick, lithe movements and the thick, lustrous dark hair that flowed out from underneath her sombrero. He couldn't see her face very well, because she kept her eyes turned shyly toward the ground and the prominent brim of the headgear was in the way. She was dressed like the man, right down to the sandals.

"I have a cabin not far from here," the man said. "Perhaps half a mile. Can you make it that far?"

Ki's hip was throbbing from the bullet crease he had suffered as he leapt onto the freight car where Jessie and Ryan had been, and pain was still hammering in his head in time to his pulse. Every muscle in his body was stiff and sore and bruised from the fall into the arroyo.

But somehow Ki managed to nod, and his voice was stronger as he said, "I can make it."

• • •

The man's name was Wayland. The Reverend Doctor Timothy Wayland, he explained as he poured a cup of pulque for Ki and slid it across the top of the rough-hewn wooden table. "I was once a Doctor of Divinity, as well as Classical Studies," Wayland said.

Ki clasped both hands around the cup and lifted it to his lips, closing his eyes as he sipped the thick, fiery liquid. He felt its warmth spreading through him, and after a moment he was able to speak again. "What happened?"

"Ah, it's an old story, my Celestial friend." Wayland patted the earthenware jug of pulque. "A fondness for the fruit of the vine led to my disgrace and downfall. I had to give up my pulpit, and from there I was seduced into all manner of sins, those of the flesh and otherwise. Finally, it seemed that the only suitable place for one who had fallen so far was a wilderness such as this one." He smiled over at Ana, who sat quietly on a bench next to the wall of the cabin. "I never dreamed that I would find my salvation among the simple people who live here."

"I didn't think much of anyone lived in these parts," Ki commented. He drank some more of the pulque.

"True, this section of the Sierra Madre is rather sparsely populated, but there are a few villages nearby where the inhabitants eke out a living by farming. And of course there are the ranches. Great ranches owned by men who rule these mountains like feudal barons of old."

Ki nodded slowly. He recalled that Don Arturo Hernandez's rancho was in these mountains, but farther to the south and west. While vegetation was sparse in places, there were also quite a few fertile valleys where horses and cattle could graze.

If he could reach Don Arturo's hacienda, he could bring back help. The old man and his entire crew would gallop into the mouth of Hell, Ki thought, if it meant rescuing Jessie and keeping Lucardo Perez from getting his filthy hands on Lucifer.

But he wasn't sure how far away Don Arturo's ranch was, nor how to go about finding it. Besides, Wayland had no horses, and it was too far to walk. Wayland didn't really have much of anything, to be honest, except this rude jacal made of mud and stone and sticks, and the meager possessions inside it.

That, and the companionship of Ana.

Ki wasn't sure how the young woman had come to share the hut with Wayland, and it probably wouldn't be polite to ask. After all, Wayland had done as good a job of patching him up as could have been expected under the conditions.

The bullet wound in Ki's arm had been cleaned and bound up with cloth, and the same was true of the crease on his hip. His body was covered with bruises and scrapes, but there didn't seem to be any other serious injuries, either external or internal. After tending to the wounds, Wayland had given Ki a wooden bowl full of some sort of stew from a big iron pot simmering over a cook fire, and the food had also done a great deal to restore Ki's strength. He was tired and felt as if he could lie down on one of the bunks and sleep for a week, but he knew now that he would be all right.

Which meant it was time to start thinking about how to go about reaching Jessie and helping her get out of whatever predicament she found herself in.

Ki pushed the cup of pulque aside, not wanting to drink too much and muddle his mind, especially not in his exhausted state. He asked Wayland, "Have you ever been to the end of that railroad spur line?"

"Where all the old mines are? I've hunted there," the man replied. "Sometimes when I'm lucky I can down a mountain goat." He patted the stock of the high-powered rifle that lay across his lap.

"Then you can take me there?"

"I suppose so. Why do you want to go there?"

Because it would be the most likely place to pick up the trail of the *bandidos,* Ki thought, and that probably meant Jessie's trail as well. He was about to launch into an explanation when he heard a deep rumble, a sound so low that it was sensed almost as much as heard, and a faint vibration came from the hard-packed dirt of the jacal floor through the soles of his feet. Ki frowned in surprise and said, "What is *that?*"

The young woman called Ana crossed herself and breathed, "*El Monte del Fuego!*"

"That means—" Wayland began.

"I know what it means," Ki said. "The Mountain of Fire."

★

Chapter 11

Corrales reached down and grasped Jessie's arm. "Allow me to help you up, señorita."

He hauled Jessie to her feet with surprising ease and at the same time plucked the guns from her holsters. There was a lot of strength packed into his broad-shouldered frame. His brothers, Lupe and Emiliano, stood off to one side, both of them looking rather concerned. Lupe mopped sweat from his face and said, "Are you certain this is a good idea, Esteban?"

"We have gone too far to back out now, *gordo!*" Corrales snapped.

"Esteban is right," Emiliano put in. "We must proceed with the plan."

Corrales slapped Emiliano on the shoulder. "The plan you devised, *mi hermano,* is a most excellent one indeed. You are a genius!"

The gaunt man shrugged in acceptance of the compliment.

Jessie was still rather breathless, but she managed to say, "What . . . what the hell is going on here?"

Corrales smiled at her. "I may have lost a race," he said, "but I have won two great prizes. One is the horse Lucifer." He pointed up the canyon, and when Jessie looked in the direction he indicated, she saw that the bandits who had ridden after Lucifer were now leading him back. Several reatas were looped around his neck, and he was coming reluctantly with the *bandidos*.

Corrales went on. "The second prize is even more important. I speak, of course, of you, Señorita Starbuck."

"It was *your* men who took over the train, not Perez's," Jessie said, awestruck by the audacity of Corrales's actions.

The rancher shrugged eloquently. "If the authorities wish to blame the attack on the train on that fool Perez, so much the better. The trail of the bandits will lead into the mountains and then disappear. No one will ever know that you and Lucifer have been taken to my hacienda."

Jessie's mouth tightened as she said, "You're insane!"

"Hardly. I am sane enough to know what I want and do whatever is necessary to take it."

At Jessie's feet, Ryan shifted a little and let out a groan. Immediately Jessie knelt beside him and said urgently, "Silencio! Silencio, are you all right?"

Ryan lifted himself onto his elbows and shook his head like a dog shaking water from its coat. He looked up, and his eyes widened in surprise at the sight of the three Corrales brothers. "What the hell . . . !" he exclaimed.

"It seems that Perez wasn't behind the attack on the train after all," Jessie explained grimly. "Señor Corrales is to blame for what happened."

And that included Ki's death, Jessie told herself. No matter what happened, even if it cost her own life, she would avenge her friend.

But revenge would have to wait. For now, Jessie knew she had to concentrate on staying alive and biding her time until the moment came to strike.

Ryan rolled over and pushed himself into a sitting position. He shook his head again. "Doesn't seem to be any bones broken," he said. "I reckon I was just knocked out for a few minutes when I landed."

"You are a lucky man," Corrales said. "You will be aware of the moment of your death, rather than having it steal upon you unawares."

Jessie looked up at him. "You'd be a fool to kill Silencio," she said coldly. "Do you think you can handle Lucifer without him?"

Corrales waved a hand at the men who had captured the black stallion. "My vaqueros seem to be doing all right."

"Sure, they can dab a loop on him and drag him," Jessie said with a shrug. "But I'd be willing to bet that none of them can ride him."

"Do you wish to wager your friend's life on that?" Corrales nodded toward Ryan.

Jessie glanced at the big redhead. "What do you think, Silencio?"

Ryan picked himself up and brushed some of the dust from his clothes. "Nobody can ride Lucifer unless I let the horse know it's all right," he declared.

"We shall see about that." Corrales turned and snapped an order in Spanish to the men holding their ropes taut on Lucifer.

Two of the vaqueros let their reatas go slack and removed the loops from Lucifer's neck with practiced flips of the wrist. That left only one man holding the stallion, and he had his hands full as Lucifer began to pull and twist against the rope.

Jessie moved closer to Ryan and asked in a low voice, "How was I supposed to run Lucifer in races if nobody can ride him without your say-so? You were only going as far as Laredo!"

"Well, I might've been exaggerating just a mite," Ryan

answered, his words equally quiet. "He's really not *that* particular about who rides him."

Jessie stared at him in disbelief. "But if one of Corrales's men is able to ride him, Corrales is liable to shoot you!"

"Could happen," Ryan admitted. "But I'm playing a hunch."

"You're betting your life on that."

"You were willing to."

Jessie grimaced. "We don't have much choice, do we?"

"Not a damned bit."

One of Corrales's men—Jessie wasn't sure whether to think of them as *bandidos* or vaqueros or both—had taken his gunbelt off and now doffed his sombrero and the short *charro* jacket he wore. He approached Lucifer with one hand out, talking softly to the horse in Spanish. Corrales watched with folded arms and an expression of approval on his face.

Jessie glanced around. Several more of the rancher's men were watching her and Ryan, and they held Winchesters ready in their hands in case of any trouble. Here in this canyon, there was nowhere to run, no point in making a break for freedom. She and Ryan would have to wait for a better time and place before they tried to escape.

Lucifer snorted and tossed his head as the man drew nearer. The horse looked wild despite the saddle on his back, and Jessie would have thought twice about approaching such an animal. Suddenly Lucifer reared and lashed out at the man with his hooves.

The man sprang back lithely and continued talking to the horse. Lucifer came down on all four legs and regarded the man curiously. As Jessie and Ryan watched anxiously, Lucifer seemed to grow less upset. The soft, crooning voice was getting to him and calming him down, Jessie thought bleakly.

"Lucifer's settling down," she hissed to Ryan.

"Yeah, he appears to be. I could give a whistle and get him stirred up again, but then Corrales would probably just have me shot."

"More than likely," Jessie agreed. "Let's wait and see how Lucifer reacts once that hombre is actually on his back."

Gradually, the vaquero worked his way around on Lucifer's left side. Keeping up the soft, singsong monologue, he reached for the saddle horn. Ryan leaned over to Jessie and said, "That fella has busted some broncs before, you can tell that."

Jessie nodded without speaking. Her throat was tight with anxiety.

Grasping the saddle horn, the vaquero swung himself easily into leather. He took up the reins and settled himself onto the saddle, then looked over at Corrales and smiled, pleased with himself.

Lucifer went berserk.

The big black stallion went from standing still to a blur of motion in the blink of an eye. He swapped ends, sunfished, kicked up his heels, and all but turned himself inside out as he fought to dislodge the unwelcome weight from his back. The vaquero yelled in fear and surprise and hung on for dear life. He raked Lucifer's flanks cruelly with the big rowels on his spurs and sawed the bit back and forth in the horse's mouth. Ryan growled and took a step forward before Jessie stopped him with a firm hand on his arm.

"Look at the way he's treating Lucifer, damn him!" Ryan complained.

"Look at the way Lucifer's treating *him*."

It was true. Daylight showed between the horse and the seat of the man's pants with alarming regularity. The vaquero slammed back down into the saddle with bone-jarring and tooth-rattling force each time Lucifer bucked. He swayed dizzingly from side to side.

Finally, after what was probably only seconds but seemed much longer, the vaquero lost his grip and went sailing through the air to land in a heap on the canyon floor. Dust billowed up around him. Lucifer trotted several feet away and then turned to regard the man contemptuously as he blew air out through his nose. The man rolled over and held up his hands, saying pitifully, *"No más! No más!"*

The confident smile had disappeared from the face of Esteban Corrales. He glared at the vaquero who had been thrown and then barked orders at the other men. They started shaking out loops in their reatas.

Lucifer didn't wait to be lassoed again. He suddenly lunged toward the mouth of the canyon, pulling tight the single rope that still held him. The rope's owner had dallied the other end around his saddle horn, drawing it snug around the flat-topped apple. He tried desperately to ease the dally and give the reata some slack, but he was too late. Lucifer hit the end of the rope with all of his weight and strength.

The tension was too much for the rawhide. The reata snapped with a sound almost like a gunshot, and suddenly Lucifer was running free.

Ryan jammed two fingers in his mouth and gave a shrill whistle. Instantly Lucifer veered toward him. The horse cut between Ryan and Jessie and the men with the rifles. Corrales shouted, "Don't shoot! Don't shoot, for God's sake!"

Lucifer never slowed down as Ryan leapt toward the saddle. The big redhead performed as smooth a running mount as any Comanche or Pony Express rider ever did. He swung up and landed hard in the saddle, and Lucifer headed for the open range outside the canyon without slackening his pace.

"Go after him and kill him!" Corrales screamed. He strode angrily over to Jessie and grabbed her arm. "I'm surprised you didn't try to go with your amigo, Señorita Starbuck."

"There wasn't time," Jessie replied curtly. Her jaw tightened as she stared after the fleeing Ryan and saw several of Corrales's men lift their rifles. She waited for the crash of the weapons. It was obvious Ryan wasn't going to reach the mouth of the canyon in time.

Without any warning, Ryan reined in. He slowed Lucifer to a trot. Quickly Corrales called out to his vaqueros, "Hold your fire!"

Ryan turned Lucifer around and rode back toward them. His face was grim as he reined to a halt in front of Corrales and Jessie and said to the rancher, "See, that's why you need me alive, Corrales. Lucifer does what I tell him to do and nothing else. Nobody else can handle him like me."

"You appear to be correct, Señor Ryan." Corrales nodded. "I will let you live . . . for now. But I warn you not to cross me or try to escape. I will have you shot down immediately, Lucifer or no Lucifer."

"I understand," Ryan said. He dismounted and came over to Jessie, leading the black stallion.

"Maybe you should have kept going," Jessie told him.

Ryan shook his head. "Not even Lucifer can outrun a bullet. And besides, you were still here. I couldn't go off and leave you."

"Quite touching," Corrales said. "But you should know, Señor Ryan, that you will no longer have anything to do with Señorita Starbuck. I did not go to all the trouble to bring her here so that you could enjoy the fruits of my labor." He snapped his fingers.

Some of the vaqueros moved between Jessie and Ryan, and there was no arguing with the rifles they carried. Ryan shrugged, and Jessie said, "Don't worry, Silencio. We'll get out of this."

Corrales just laughed coldly at her words. He took her arm again and led her over to a chestnut mare that was saddled and waiting.

"I brought this horse for you, señorita," he said. "You will please mount up and ride with us."

"I don't have any choice, do I?"

"None at all, my dear."

Jessie started to correct him—she was nobody's dear, let alone his—but she decided not to waste her breath. She mounted the chestnut while Corrales and his brothers also climbed onto their horses. Lupe looked definitely uncomfortable in the saddle, but obviously he went where Esteban and Emiliano did. Corrales gestured to some of his men, and they moved out into the lead, taking Ryan and Lucifer with them. Outnumbered and outgunned the way he was, there was nothing Ryan could do except go along with their wishes.

Corrales gave Jessie a little bow and gestured for her to precede him. "Shall we go?"

Jessie jogged her mount into a walk. As she started up the canyon, Corrales fell in beside her. Lupe and Emiliano brought up the rear.

For several minutes, Jessie rode in silence. Then, her curiosity getting the better of her, she said, "I don't understand this. Repairing that spur line and the switch to throw the train over onto it took some time and effort. You never even saw me before yesterday, Corrales."

The rancher laughed. "That is not strictly true. But I had seen Lucifer, and I knew he was to be sold to someone from your country. I did not intend to allow such a horse to leave Mexico."

"Then you were out to steal Lucifer all along, and I just

happened to be thrown in on the deal." Jessie couldn't help but sound a little bitter.

"I promise you, señorita, that once I saw you in Monterrey, I knew I had to have you. That was not yesterday, however. I was at the Hotel Condor when you arrived the day before that."

Jessie's breath caught in her throat. "Those men who jumped Ki and me when we were on our way to the restaurant—"

"Were in my employ," Corrales admitted. "They were supposed to capture you and bring you to me. I acted rashly, so overwhelmed was I by your beauty. Once I thought about it and consulted with my brothers, I decided to combine my plan to liberate Lucifer, which was already under way, with my desire to have you for my own."

"Steal a horse and kidnap a woman at the same time," Jessie muttered. "Well, I guess you're efficient, anyway, even if you are a murderous bastard."

Corrales chuckled, obviously taking no offense at her harsh words.

Jessie went on. "Those men who tried to grab Lucifer at the racecourse yesterday . . . I take it they worked for you, too?"

"Not at all," Corrales said with a shake of his head. "Those were really some of Perez's men, I believe. Perez is crude, like most *bandidos,* but he is daring. He would not have hesitated to try to steal Lucifer in Monterrey."

"But you were lucky and he failed."

"Fortune always smiles on me," Corrales said with a smile of his own.

Not always, Jessie vowed to herself. Sooner or later, Corrales's plan was going to blow up right in his face.

And she intended to be there when it happened.

★

Chapter 12

"The Mountain of Fire," Ki repeated. "What is it? A volcano?"

"An excellent guess, my young friend," Wayland said. "The Sierra Madres are volcanic in nature, after all, and were formed by a series of eruptions and upheavals ages ago. Most of the volcanoes are now dead, of course, or at least inactive. A few are simply dormant most of the time, however, and occasionally they still spew forth some steam and shake the ground, just to remind everyone how pitiful all of man's efforts really are compared to the forces of nature."

"Does this Monte del Fuego erupt very often?"

Wayland shook his head. "There hasn't been a full-scale eruption in the time I've been in this region. Ana's people, though, tell stories of how the mountain breathed fire and sent waves of burning, deadly destruction down its sides. A lava flow, of course. I've studied the lava deposits and would estimate the last real eruption took place at least a couple of hundred years ago."

Ki frowned and said, "But the stories—"

"Could have easily been passed down from generation to generation for that long," Wayland interrupted.

Ki nodded as he mulled over what the man had told him. It was entirely possible Wayland was right about the timing of the last eruption, he decided. Ki was familiar with volcanoes; Mount Fuji, in his homeland of Japan, was volcanic, after all, and although it had been over a hundred and seventy years since its last eruption, Mexico was not the only place where stories were handed down over the generations. Ki had heard how the lava and deadly gases spewed forth by the volcano had killed many of his countrymen.

And he also knew that such eruptions were sometimes preceded by small earth tremors, such as the one that had shaken Wayland's hut a few minutes earlier.

But those tremors could go on for years, even decades, before the actual eruption took place, so there was no way of predicting exactly what was going to happen. He could not allow himself to be distracted by such considerations, either. The only thing that mattered was finding Jessie and rescuing her from Perez.

"If you will take me to the end of the spur line tomorrow," he said to Wayland, "I would be in your debt, Doctor."

"Please, my friend, don't call me that. Those days are far in the past and will never come again. Just call me Timothy."

Ki nodded gravely. "Very well, Timothy."

"But are you sure you want to go to the old mines tomorrow? So soon? You should rest for a few days and let your injuries heal."

"I cannot take that much time," Ki said with a shake of his head. "I must find a friend of mine who was on that train when it was captured by Lucardo Perez."

"Perez!" Wayland exclaimed, and Ana looked frightened and crossed herself, much as she had done when the little earthquake shook the jacal.

"I believe it was his band of thieves who captured the train and killed many of the people on it."

"Yes, Perez and his men would do that," Wayland muttered, as much to himself as to Ki. He lifted his gaunt face and looked at the visitor. "But what can one man do against the likes of Perez?"

"All men have weaknesses. All that is required is to locate them. Does Perez bother you here?"

Wayland shook his head. "He demands tribute from the villages, but someone like me, an old man living alone save for Ana, Perez knows that I have nothing of value to him. I have seen him and his men riding by in the distance, but they have never come here."

"What about the ranches?"

"The smaller ones, he raids. The larger ones, like the rancho belonging to the Corrales brothers, he leaves alone. Perez already has the *rurales* looking for him, although the *rurales* don't really have a chance of finding him up in the mountains. He doesn't want any extra trouble."

"Corrales," Ki repeated with a frown. "That ranch is near here?"

"Not too near. Perhaps ten miles away, across the mountains. Why?"

"I know Esteban Corrales. He might help me if I could reach his hacienda."

Wayland shuddered and shook his head. "The Corrales brothers are evil men. I would not ask them for help."

"Well, I have to admit that I wasn't too impressed with them myself when I met them," Ki said. "But they might be better than nothing."

Ana said something, the spate of Spanish words coming so rapidly from her mouth that Ki could not keep up with them. He turned to look at her. Now that they were inside the hut, she had removed the wide-brimmed sombrero, and

99

he could see her face in the light from the little lantern on the table. It was an attractive face, with skin the color of honey and fairly regular features, with discernible Indio traces. Wayland nodded patiently as she continued chattering at him.

When Ana finally fell silent, Wayland turned to Ki and said, "She doesn't think you should go anywhere near the Corrales rancho. She says the Corrales brothers have done bad things to her people, and I believe her. She says she would sooner take her chances with Perez."

"She wouldn't think so if she had been on that train with me," Ki muttered. "But I'll think about it. If there is some other way that doesn't involve Corrales and his brothers, I will try to follow that path."

"Good." Wayland stood up and rested a hand on Ki's shoulder. "Now you must rest. No matter what you do tomorrow, you have to have some sleep tonight."

"You're right," Ki admitted.

"You can take my bunk. I often sleep out under the stars."

"I don't want to put you out—"

"Nonsense. I wouldn't have offered if I hadn't meant it, my friend. Please."

Ki glanced at the bunk. The mattress on it was only a pad of straw ticking, but at the moment it looked as irresistible to Ki as the finest four-poster feather bed in the fanciest hotel in Austin. It seemed to be calling out to him in a siren song of promised slumber.

He nodded. "Thank you, Timothy. I won't forget all you have done for me."

"You've honored us with your company, my boy. That's repayment enough. Come along, Ana."

Wayland picked up some blankets and led the young woman outside. Ki watched them go, still feeling slightly guilty, then blew out the lamp and headed for the bunk. He stretched out on it gratefully, wincing a little as his still-sore muscles complained.

And that was the last thing he remembered as sleep claimed him.

He came awake instantly at the gentle touch.

"Sssh." The hand moved from his groin to his chest and pressed firmly as he started to sit up. The soft voice continued. "It is Ana."

Ki blinked and gave a little shake of his head. He was disgusted with himself. No matter how tired he was, no matter how much he had been through in the past twenty-four hours, there was no excuse for letting her sneak up on him like this. He should have awakened as soon as she entered the hut, no matter how cat-footed she moved. And what the hell was she doing now?

Well, he knew *what* she was doing, of course. She was moving her hand back down his chest, unfastening the buttons of his shirt along the way. But he didn't know why.

Rapidly she made her intentions so plain that even someone as battered and groggy as Ki was at this moment could understand them. When her fingers reached the waistband of his pants, she tugged his shirt free from it and then went after those buttons. She got them undone with a few deft motions, then returned her hand to his muscular chest.

She spread her fingers and rubbed her palm over his skin, moving in ever-widening circles that soon had her brushing her hand over his nipples. She moved lower and lower, spreading his shirt open as she went. Her hand was work-roughened, but Ki didn't notice. Under the circumstances, her palm felt as smooth as velvet to him.

But no matter how pleasant what she was doing felt to him, there were definite limits as to how far he would abuse a host's hospitality. He reached down and caught Ana's wrist, stopping her caresses. "You should not be doing this," he whispered, not sure how much English she actually understood.

Evidently quite a bit, even though she didn't speak it as well, because she said, "Timothy not mind. He be glad I bring you pleasure—if he know."

"You're his woman, aren't you?"

"Not like that. He . . . he buy me from my father to help him here, to cook for him. Maybe he want me, too, but that part of him . . ." Ki heard the soft swish of her long hair in the darkness as she shook her head. "It not work anymore. Not good enough, anyway."

Ki frowned. He still wasn't sure he would be doing the right thing by taking advantage of what the young woman was offering him. But he could not deny that her touch had had an effect on him. His staff was rock-hard and pressing rather painfully against the front of his pants.

He reached out toward Ana, and what he found made up his mind for him. His hand was filled with the soft warmth of a naked breast, the large nipple erect and wanting. Ana gasped at his touch, but she didn't pull back. In fact, she leaned forward so that more of the globe of flesh was pressed into his hand.

She pulled his pants down around his hips so that his manhood sprang free. It was a relief to be released from the confines of his clothes, but he discovered a second later than even more exquisite tortures awaited. She fisted both hands loosely around the shaft and began sliding them up and down, exclaiming quietly in Spanish at the length and heft of his organ.

Ki's hips thrust up involuntarily at her touch, and he

moaned from a combination of lust and pain as his sore muscles protested vigorously at the slightest movement. "I do not know if I can do this, Ana," he said regretfully.

"You not have to do anything," she told him. "I do it all."

With that, she bent over and took him into her mouth. His eyes had adjusted now to the faint starlight coming in through the hut's single window. There was just enough illumination for him to make out the dark cloud of her raven hair as it spread out around her head and blanketed his midsection. Her warm, wet lips closed on his manhood, encircling the shaft maddeningly. As her head bobbed up and down, Ki forced himself to remain motionless except for his right hand, which stroked the velvety softness of her bare back as she leaned over him.

He could tell she had had little experience, but that did not matter. She was allowing instinct and desire to tell her what to do. Ki's breath came faster and harsher in his throat as she used her lips and tongue on him. She gripped the shaft with one hand while the other stole between his legs to cup and fondle his sac.

When he was afraid his climax was about to blast out into the hot cavern of her mouth, she abruptly took her lips away. Ki almost groaned in frustration at being denied release. But in the next instant, she swung a leg over him and knelt above him on the bunk. She gripped his organ and tucked the head of it between the moisture-drenched lips of her slit. She hesitated, took a deep breath, and then lowered herself onto him.

The breath came out of her in a low cry. Ki lifted his hands to her heavy breasts and cupped them, flicking the erect nipples with his thumbs. Ana's hips thrust back and forth frenziedly. Her wanting was too strong for her to go slow any longer.

Despite the pain in his body, Ki lifted himself from the bunk and met her thrusts with jabs of his own as she pumped him. He, as well, was too aroused to delay. So many times in the recent past he had been within a whisker's breadth of death.

Tonight he was embracing life.

He felt his climax wash over him. His back arched and his grip on Ana's breasts tightened as he poured forth his juices into her. Spasm after spasm shook him. Ana cried out, so loudly that Wayland had to hear her outside. Ki was beyond caring. He dropped his hands to Ana's hips and held her tightly in place as he drove into her even deeper than before, to conclude his orgasm. She fell forward onto his chest, gasping for breath.

Ki was out of breath himself. He slid his arms around Ana and held her tightly as his pulse gradually slowed and enough air finally returned to his lungs. He felt several delicious little shudders go through Ana's body, aftereffects of her own climax.

The tremors were something like the vibrations he had felt earlier, the vibrations that emanated from the volcano known as the Mountain of Fire. There was one big difference, however.

These tremors came *after* an eruption, rather than before.

With that thought in his head and a smile on his face, Ki went back to sleep.

★

Chapter 13

It was slow going over the mountains. The trail led through canyons, up and down switchbacks over passes, and along ledges with sheer rock walls on one side and yawning gulfs on the other. Jessie had no idea how far away Corrales's ranch was, but as nightfall drew nearer, she decided that they probably couldn't reach it before dark. That would mean camping out on the trail.

She was wrong about that, however. The group of riders ascended a particularly steep pass, and when they reached the top, the vaqueros in front pulled their horses to the side and halted, waiting for Jessie, Corrales, and the rancher's brothers to catch up.

Jessie glanced at Corrales, who motioned for her to go ahead. She hesitated, then urged the chestnut mare on. There was a broad, open space at the head of the pass, and Jessie didn't rein in until she reached it.

But then, almost overwhelmed by what she saw, she brought the mare to a stop and looked out over the valley spread before her. She would never have expected to find such a place in these rocky, rugged mountains.

It was like a little slice of paradise, bright green in the glow of the setting sun. The floor of the valley was carpeted with lush grass and dotted with pine trees. The fading sunlight winked on the surface of a stream that meandered along roughly through the center of the valley. Jessie saw horses and cattle grazing, and on the far side of the valley were cultivated fields.

The most impressive sight was at the other end of the valley, however. A tall, snowcapped mountain reared toward the heavens there, and about a quarter of the way up its slope was one of the most magnificent houses Jessie had ever seen. Huge and sprawling, constructed of adobe and whitewashed timbers and a red slate roof, the place was more mansion than house. Even at this distance, Jessie could tell that it was surrounded by beautiful, elaborate gardens.

"Welcome to my home," Esteban Corrales said softly beside her.

"It . . . it's beautiful," Jessie said in spite of herself.

"Indeed it is," Corrales agreed. "My brothers and I found it some fifteen years ago, when we were being pursued through this part of the Sierra Madre by the *rurales*."

Jessie glanced over at him. "You were outlaws?"

"I prefer to think we were revolutionaries. But we decided that it would be even more profitable to change our names and become ranchers, especially with such a magnificent place for the taking. No one lived here then except for a few farmers."

"What happened to them?"

"They work now for me," Corrales said. "The ones who were willing to be reasonable, that is."

A wave of coldness went through Jessie. "You killed the others, didn't you?"

Corrales shrugged and said, "They were peons. They could not be allowed to stand in the way of my destiny."

She felt a surge of revulsion for the man. He might be handsome, and he was undeniably wealthy and powerful . . .

106

but there was nothing inside him, no more soul than might be found in a snake or a scorpion. She sensed that his brothers were the same way.

"I am glad you find my valley pleasant," Corrales went on, "since it will be your home, as well, for the rest of your days."

Silencio Ryan spoke up. "I wouldn't count on that, Corrales," he called over.

Idly Corrales flicked a wrist, and one of the vaqueros slammed the butt of a rifle into the small of Ryan's back. Ryan gasped and leaned forward over the neck of the big black stallion, agony etched on his face. He had to hold tightly to the saddle horn to keep from falling off.

Angrily, Jessie said, "You won't win my affection by mistreating my friends, Corrales."

The rancher shrugged languidly. "I care less about winning your affection, Señorita Starbuck, than I do about possessing it. As long as you arc in my hands, you have no choice in the matter."

"We'll see about that," Jessie said ominously.

"Indeed we will. Now, let us go."

Corrales led the procession down into the verdant valley with Jessie riding at his side, unwilling though she might have been. For the moment, Corrales still held all the cards, and she knew it.

The sun had dipped behind the rounded mountains to the west by the time the group of riders reached the floor of the valley. Shadows gathered quickly as dusk closed in. It was not difficult, though, to follow the trail leading to the huge house at the other end of the valley. The path was broad and well defined. Above the riders, the sky shaded from blue to purple to violet, and as the violet faded to black, the twinkle of stars began to appear, like diamonds on stygian velvet. Up ahead, on the mountainside, the mansion blazed with lights. Obviously the master of the house was expected.

It was fully dark by the time they reached the path that led up to the hacienda. Corrales called a halt, drew a pistol from his belt, and fired it into the air. That was some sort of signal, Jessie figured, and a couple of minutes later, she saw that her guess was right. More lights appeared, these bobbing and weaving as they came down the path from the house.

They were servants carrying torches, Jessie saw as the lights came closer. Dozens of servants, so that when they were all in position with the blazing, pitch-soaked torches held high above their heads, the entire path leading up to the house was brightly lit. Corrales urged his horse into a walk and motioned for Jessie to ride beside him.

The path was wide enough for two horses abreast. Jessie rode along the inside of the trail, next to the rock wall. The path twisted and turned, and as they rode higher and higher, Jessie found herself wondering if she could crowd her horse against Corrales's without warning and force him off the edge. That was possible, she decided, but without Corrales there, likely all it would get her would be a bullet in the back from one of his men. She thought about Lupe and Emiliano; neither of them would protect her, she knew. Neither of them looked at her with the same desire in his eyes as Esteban did. Besides, he was the undoubted leader here. If he were dead, it was unlikely his brothers could control the wild cutthroats bringing up the rear of the procession.

Like it or not, she couldn't strike back at Corrales just yet. The time was coming, though, she told herself. The time was coming. . . .

It took quite a while to reach the broad shelf on the side of the mountain where the mansion was located. When they came to the top of the path and emerged onto the shelf, Jessie got her first close look at the house. It was even more impressive than it had appeared from a distance. The structure rose three stories high and was surrounded by extravagant gardens, as she had noted earlier. There were huge double doors of ornately carved hardwood at the entrance, and they were open at the moment to reveal a large courtyard within. In the center of the courtyard was a fountain, and Jessie could hear water flowing in it, tinkling like the music of a softly strummed guitar.

"You will be happy here, Jessica," Corrales said as he reined up in front of the entrance. "You will see."

Tight-lipped, Jessie made no reply. This was a world of Corrales's own making, and nothing she could say would convince him how empty and illusory his fantasies were.

Corrales stepped down from the saddle and extended a hand to her. "Allow me to assist you," he said. He was trying to be as charming as all get-out, Jessie thought bitterly, and what was even worse, she had to play along with him for the time being.

She dismounted, taking his hand as she stepped away from the mare. A glance over her shoulder told her that Lupe and Emiliano were getting off their horses, too, but the vaqueros, along with Silencio Ryan still riding in their midst, were heading around the wall of the estate toward the rear of the vast hacienda. There would be quarters back there for them, Jessie figured, and obviously they planned to keep Ryan with them as a prisoner. He would not likely be allowed into the main house.

Corrales was treating *her* like an honored guest, however. He bowed low and said, "Welcome to my casa, señorita. I hope you enjoy your stay."

"*Gracias,*" Jessie forced herself to say. She even summoned up a faint smile from somewhere. Might as well let him think he was winning her over with his charm

109

and wealth, she decided. That might lull him into making a mistake.

And all it would take was one. . . .

If the outside of the house was breathtaking, the inside was even more so. As the heir of the vast Starbuck business empire, Jessie had traveled in the circles of the rich and powerful for years, had dined with robber barons and heads of state, had visited the royal courts of Europe, had seen just about all there was to see when it came to downright fancy places.

Or so she had thought.

The house of Esteban Corrales was an eye-opener.

Thick woven rugs of incredible beauty were on the floor, which was of highly polished hardwood. Furniture that could have graced a French king's castle was scattered around the huge, high-ceilinged rooms. Most of an entire wall in one room was taken up by a massive fireplace. Jessie saw a multitude of paintings and sculptures, and although her eye was not well trained in art, she would have been willing to bet that every one of them was an original and priceless.

Corrales noticed her looking at the paintings and said, "Many of them are supposedly lost treasures that I had smuggled out of Europe. There are crowned heads who would almost give up their thrones for what I have accumulated here."

"And yet you steal a race horse and kidnap a woman." Jessie couldn't stop herself from making the comment.

Corrales's shoulders rose and fell. "There are treasures, Jessica, and then there are *treasures*. You and Lucifer fall into the latter category."

"I suppose I should be honored."

"Indeed you should."

As far as Jessie could tell, they were alone in the house except for a white-haired old majordomo and a couple of young, scared-looking maids. Lupe and Emiliano had left after a low-voiced conversation with their brother. There was no one here to whom she could appeal for help.

Corrales had something in mind for tonight, and Jessie had no trouble guessing what it was. After a quick tour of the ground floor, he said to her, "One of the maids will take you up to your room now. You will find that a bath has been drawn for you, and clothes have been laid out. I hope you approve of them."

"You got ready for me in a hurry."

"No offense, *querida,* but you are not the first lady to visit me here. The loveliest, without a shadow of a doubt, but not the first."

"I see," Jessie said coolly, wondering if Corrales's other "visitors" had been terrified young women from the farming families that had inhabited this valley before the arrival of the brothers. She decided that was highly probable.

Corrales smiled at her and then turned to call, "Juanita!"

One of the timid-looking maids came into the room. "*Sí,* Señor Esteban?"

"Take Señorita Starbuck up to the chamber which has been prepared for her," Corrales ordered. "I want you to be of any assistance to her that you can."

"*Sí,* Señor Esteban," Juanita said without looking up at him. She went to the doorway of the room and waited, her hands clasped behind her back.

Corrales looked at Jessie and waved a hand for her to accompany the maid. Jessie hesitated only a second, then did so. Arguing wasn't going to accomplish anything.

Juanita led her up a broad, curving staircase. The steps were white marble, and so was the balustrade. Tiny flecks of color sparkled in the stone.

111

When the two women reached the second floor, Juanita took Jessie along a balcony to another set of hardwood double doors. Corrales had spared no expense in building this place. He had been on the run from the law when he found the valley, he had said, and Jessie wondered what his crimes had been. Whatever they were, they must have been lucrative, because no one could put together a place like this without having plenty of money to start with.

Juanita opened the doors and ushered Jessie into another luxuriously appointed room. This one had a huge, four-poster bed with a silk drape over it. There were thick rugs underfoot here, too, as well as more exquisite paintings. A large, claw-footed bathtub had been carried into the room and filled with hot water. Steam rose from the surface of the water. After all she had been through, Jessie had to admit that the prospect of sinking down into that bathtub for a nice long soak sounded incredibly appealing.

"The señorita wishes for to take a bath?" Juanita asked diffidently.

"The señorita sure does," Jessie replied as she reached for the buttons of her shirt.

She might as well enjoy herself, she decided, while she waited for her chance to kill that son of a bitch Esteban Corrales.

★

Chapter 14

Hot water had never felt so good, Jessie thought. She soaked in the tub for a long time, luxuriating in the heat, until the water finally cooled. Then she rinsed off the dust that had accumulated on her body from the train ride and the horseback journey across the mountains. She washed her hair as well, submerging her head and then coming up to shake it vigorously.

Juanita had left earlier, taking Jessie's soiled and dusty clothes with her. Fresh clothing was spread out on the comforter of the big four-poster. Jessie had paid particular attention as the maid was leaving, and she had heard the faint clicking sound as Juanita locked the door. A glance at the big, arched windows on the other side of the room told Jessie that they were covered with an elaborate grillwork of black wrought iron. A lot prettier than the gray bars of a jail cell, Jessie thought, but just as effective.

She stood up and stepped out of the tub onto the rug. A large, thick towel was draped over the back of a nearby chair. Jessie picked it up and wrapped herself in it, and as she did so, the door of the room opened and Juanita hurried in, pausing only to close and relock the door behind her. The maid must have been watching through the keyhole, Jessie decided.

"I will do that for you, señorita," Juanita offered.

Jessie shook her head. "I can dry myself off, thanks."

"Then I will assist you in your dressing." She sounded almost desperate to do something to help.

Jessie wrapped the towel tighter around her and tucked the end of it into the valley between her breasts. She took a close look at Juanita. The young woman was pretty, with lustrous black hair and fine features. She wore a long black skirt embroidered with elaborate red and yellow designs, and a low-cut white blouse that revealed the upper swells of her high, firm breasts. Jessie played a hunch.

"Juanita," she said quietly, "were you once the woman of Esteban Corrales?"

"Ah, señorita—" Juanita looked pained and obviously didn't want to answer.

"Tell me," Jessie said, her voice a little sharper now.

Juanita hesitated a few more seconds, then abruptly her head bobbed up and down. "All of the maids who work here in the house have shared his bed," she said miserably. "That is how he chooses us. He comes to the farms of our fathers and picks out the girl that appeals most to him. Then we come here for to live and serve him."

"I thought so. Did you have the hot bath and the pretty clothes to wear?"

"*Sí.*" The young woman's voice sounded almost wistful now. "I never thought to wear such clothes, or to sleep in such a bed . . . Don Esteban was . . . was kind to me."

"But that ended, didn't it?"

"He grew tired of me," Juanita said with a tiny shrug. "It was my fault for not exciting him any longer. But he is a generous master and allows me to remain here as his servant."

"And when he grows tired of me, I suppose I'll wind up in the same boat."

"Oh, no!" Juanita exclaimed as she looked up at Jessie. "A beautiful señorita such as yourself . . . Don Esteban will surely never grow tired of you!"

Jessie wasn't so sure of that, but it wasn't really something with which she had to concern herself, either.

She didn't intend to be here long enough for Corrales to grow tired of her.

She smiled at Juanita and stepped toward the bed. "Come on. You can help me with the clothes."

A lacy corset and some petticoats were the only undergarments Corrales had provided. Jessie tossed the towel over the back of the chair and slipped into the corset. With a figure like hers, she didn't really need to be pinched and squeezed into such a garment, so she cinched it loosely, then stepped into the petticoats. Before putting on the silk gown of sky blue, she allowed Juanita to brush out her hair. Then, while Juanita held the gown, Jessie wiggled into it from underneath. It was tight, and it lovingly outlined the proud thrust of her breasts. Jessie held her breath while Juanita fastened the buttons in the back. Maybe she should have laced that corset a little tighter after all, Jessie thought with a faint smile.

"Now there is this for you," Juanita said when she was finished with the dress. She went to a long dressing table with a mirror mounted above it and opened a small box that was lying on the table. When she turned around again, Jessie saw that she had a necklace in her hands.

But not just any necklace. This one sparkled blindingly with diamonds and emeralds and other precious stones. Involuntarily Jessie caught her breath. The necklace was one of the most beautiful pieces of jewelry she had ever seen.

Juanita held the necklace up. "You like?" she asked.

"How could I not like it? Except, of course, for the fact

that it comes from a snake like Corrales."

The maid's eyes widened. "Oh, no, you must not talk like that about Don Esteban! He is a good man, a kind man. He wants only what is best for you, señorita."

Despite what she was saying, there was a hint of desperation in Juanita's voice. More than desperation, Jessie decided. Fear, pure fear. She was afraid that someone was listening in somehow to their conversation, and if she failed to defend Corrales, that fact would be reported back to him. Such a thing was entirely possible, Jessie thought. She wouldn't put much of anything past Corrales after what she had already seen of his ruthlessness.

"I'm sorry," she told Juanita. She went over to the servant and turned her back, bending her knees a little so that the slightly shorter Juanita could loop the necklace around her throat. Juanita fastened the catch.

"Turn around and look at yourself, señorita," she urged. "You are truly beautiful."

Jessie turned and studied her image in the mirror. She had never been particularly vain, but even she had to admit that she looked pretty good, especially considering the ordeal she had endured during the past day. Her hair was still slightly damp, but it was drying quickly in the thin air of this high mountain valley. The copper-blond strands had more curl to them than usual, too.

And the necklace set off her green eyes stunningly. She looked at it for a moment, raising one hand to lightly touch the gems with her fingers, then glanced over at Juanita. "Did you wear this necklace when you were Corrales's woman?"

She shook her head rapidly. "Oh, no, señorita. That necklace is for ladies only to wear, not the daughter of a farmer. Don Esteban gave me a string of pearls for to wear, and I was very happy with them."

"You'd look good in this necklace, too." Jessie's hand went to the catch at the back of her neck. "Maybe you'd like to try it on . . ."

"No, señorita. *Por favor,* no."

Jessie realized she was frightening the young woman. "All right, Juanita," she said quickly. "You've been very kind to me, and I intend to tell Don Esteban that you've taken very good care of me."

"Really, señorita? *Gracias, gracias.*" She was so grateful that it was almost embarrassing, Jessie thought.

"What am I supposed to do now?"

"Don Esteban is waiting for you downstairs. He has had a fine meal prepared for you."

And she was more than ready for it, Jessie realized. It had been a damned long time since she and Ryan had bought tamales from the woman on the train for their lunch. So much had happened since then that it seemed difficult to believe less than twelve hours had passed.

Juanita unlocked the door again, looking apologetic as she did so, and led Jessie downstairs to a dining room with a mahogany table where forty men could have sat comfortably. Instead, Esteban Corrales waited alone at the far end. The table was set for only two diners. Jessie's place was at the right hand of Corrales.

He stood and smiled at her as she entered the room. "Ah, Jessica, you look even more lovely than I would have dreamed possible," he said. His voice became much more curt as he went on. "You may go, Juanita."

The maid ducked out of the room quickly and shut the doors behind her. Corrales sauntered down the length of the table and held out his hand to Jessie.

"Allow me," he murmured.

She took his hand without hesitation, and they walked together along the table, back to the places that had been

117

set for dinner. Wineglasses of the finest crystal had already been filled from a large, heavy bottle that stood on the table. There were platters of food in the center of the table, not the usual enchiladas and tamales and frijoles, but rather roasted duck with a glazed sauce brushed on it, elegantly small potatoes, new peas, fruit, and pastries.

Jessie raised an eyebrow at the feast. "Don't tell me you laid out this spread for Lucifer and I just happened to come along," she said.

Corrales chuckled. "This was prepared for you and you alone, *querida*. I gave instructions to my cook and housekeeper this morning to prepare a special meal for a special guest, because, you see, by that time you had been included in my plans for the day."

"You were that confident your bandits would be able to capture the train?"

"Of course. None of my men would ever disappoint me."

If they did, Corrales would probably kill them out of hand, Jessie thought.

He held a high-backed chair for her and waited until she was comfortable before taking his own seat. He clapped his hands, and the white-haired majordomo materialized from somewhere to serve the food. The old man filled Jessie's plate first, then Corrales's. When he was finished and had withdrawn, Corrales picked up his wineglass and held it out toward Jessie.

"To us," he said, an expectant look on his face.

Jessie swallowed hard and picked up her own glass. There was a definite limit as to how far she would play along with this madness, but she supposed she hadn't reached it yet. She clinked her glass against Corrales's and smiled, but she didn't say anything.

The wine was good, she had to admit that, and so was

the food. Jessie was practical-minded enough so that when she was hungry, she ate, regardless of the company, and she enjoyed this meal and didn't stop until she'd had enough. Corrales carried most of the conversation, bragging on what a fine place he had and all the things he owned.

Jessie got a definite feeling that he now considered her one of those possessions.

The majordomo brought them snifters of brandy when they were finished with the food, and as they sipped the liquor, Jessie was curious enough to ask a question that had been bothering her.

"What are you going to do with Lucifer? You can't race him. Everyone would recognize him and know that you stole him."

"This is unfortunately true. But I can ride him myself, here on my rancho, and know that no one in all of Mexico has a better horse."

"That's important enough for you to kill a bunch of innocent people?"

"When I want something, no obstacle is too great." Corrales took a cigar from his pocket, rolled it between his palms for a moment, and then leaned forward to hold the tip in the flame of one of the candles that lit the table. He puffed the tightly rolled cylinder of tobacco into life. As he leaned back in his chair, he went on. "And I also plan to breed Lucifer with my finest mares. He will improve the bloodline of my stock immensely."

Jessie couldn't deny that. Lucifer would be a welcome addition to the bloodline of any horse. But it still made a cold chill go through her to think that Corrales was willing to sacrifice so many lives for such a comparatively small gain.

But nearly all gains were small when compared to the loss of innocent lives, she mused. And it was difficult to quantify evil. Small evils were often just as bad as larger ones.

Corrales stood up. "Come with me onto the terrace," he said. He held out a hand to her once again.

She took it, and they walked through French doors onto a terrace paved with flagstones. A low marble railing ran around its edge. There was a healthy drop on the other side of that rail, Jessie saw as they drew nearer. This terrace was on the side of the house. The lower slopes of the mountain fell away to their right, while to the left the heights soared seemingly all the way to the heavens. The mountain blotted out the stars in a large portion of the sky, but at night it was impossible to see the top of it. It existed only as a dark, looming, threatening bulk, a patch of even deeper darkness.

The terrace was lit by small lanterns in the trees that grew there in huge earthenware pots. Corrales strode all the way to the railing and turned to put his back to it as he faced Jessie. Behind him, she could make out a few lights coming from the crude huts in the valley.

If she lunged toward him, she thought, and planted her hands in the middle of his chest and shoved as hard as she could, she could push him right over that railing. He wouldn't stop bouncing for a long time on his way down to the floor of the valley.

As if he were reading her mind, Corrales grinned around the cigar in his mouth and said, "If anything happens to me, Jessica, you would not live to see the sun come up tomorrow, and neither would your friend Ryan. My brothers and my men would see to that."

"I don't know what you're talking about," Jessie lied.

"I think we both know." Corrales took the cigar from his mouth and waved it, the tip glowing bright red in the air. "But no matter. I know women, and you are too intrigued by me now to try anything so foolish." He took a step toward her. "You want me, don't you, Jessica?"

He was truly insane, she thought. But she evaded his question by saying, "What I really want is to go back to that room you gave me and get some rest. It's been a very long day, as you well know."

"So you wish to go to bed." Corrales nodded smugly. "An excellent idea. I will accompany you."

"I didn't mean—" Jessie began.

He stopped her by stepping even closer and putting a hand on her shoulder. "I think we can both use a taste of what is to come."

He pulled her to him and his mouth came down, hard and ruthless, on hers.

Jessie pulled away. "No!" she said, unable to control her emotions any longer. "Don't touch me again, you bastard, or I'll—"

Corrales tossed his cigar away and lunged toward her. As he grabbed her and jerked her toward him, he growled, "You are in no position to give orders, Señorita Starbuck. If I want you, I shall take you—right here on the terrace!"

His fingers hooked in the bodice of her gown and ripped down violently, freeing her breasts from both the dress and the corset underneath. Jessie balled a fist and swung it at his head as his fingers dug cruelly into the soft flesh of her bosom. Corrales blocked the punch, cursed, and jammed his mouth down on hers again. Jessie was just about to bring her knee up into his groin as hard as she could. . . .

That was when the noise and the vibrations slammed into both of them, and the sky turned red.

★

Chapter 15

The earth shuddered so violently that Jessie was thrown off her feet. She sprawled on the flagstones of the terrace while Corrales had to grab the railing to steady himself and stay upright. From where Jessie lay, she could look up and see the top of the mountain looming over the hacienda. A hellish red glow filled the sky above the peak.

"My God!" Jessie exclaimed as the rumbling died away. "That's a volcano!"

"*Sí,*" Corrales said. "The natives of the valley call it the Mountain of Fire."

"And you built your house right under it?" Jessie asked in disbelief. She was so shaken that she had completely forgotten about her breasts revealed by the ripped gown.

Corrales reached down toward her. "The mountain has not erupted in hundreds of years. It rumbles and lights up the sky like that every so often just to remind us that it still lives."

Jessie took his hand and let him help her back to her feet. She looked down at her breasts, remembering what had been going on before nature's interruption. Her bare nipples were erect and pebbled, not from arousal but from the night air. She pulled the gown up over her bosom and held it in place. Corrales seemed to have forgotten that he had been attacking her, and she was thankful for that.

"You're insane to stay here," she said bluntly. "That volcano is the reason there were so few people living in this valley when you stumbled onto it. The farmers know they're risking their lives to stay so close to it."

Corrales shrugged. "Life is a risk, is it not, Jessica? And when the prize is a beautiful valley such as this . . . well, the risk is worthwhile."

"It wouldn't be to me."

"Yes, but you have no choice in the matter, do you?" Corrales took a deep breath. "You can return to your room. Some of the peasants still believe that angry spirits live inside the Mountain of Fire. Perhaps those spirits were trying to tell me something."

"To let Silencio and me go?" Jessie suggested.

Corrales shook his head. "The spirits would not meddle to that extent in the affairs of humans." He took Jessie's arm. "Come."

After leading Jessie back into the dining room, Corrales clapped his hands, and Juanita appeared. The maid looked pale and shaken, and Jessie guessed that the tremor had upset her. Juanita had grown up in this valley, and she might well be one of those of whom Corrales had spoken. She might believe that there were spirits inside the mountain, showing by shaking the earth and spitting fire into the sky their displeasure with the puny humans who had dared to build a house in their domain.

"Take Señorita Starbuck back to her room," Corrales ordered.

Juanita nodded. "*Sí*, señor."

Jessie went out through the large doors of the dining room as Juanita stood to one side. It was a little difficult to maintain one's dignity while holding a shredded gown over nearly bare breasts, but Jessie tried. She remembered how to get back to the room Corrales had set aside for her, and could have managed even without Juanita leading the way, eyes downcast. But Juanita was as much guard as guide, Jessie knew, and she didn't want to get the young woman into any trouble by not cooperating.

When they were back in the bedroom upstairs and Juanita was turning away toward the door—to lock it behind her when she left, undoubtedly—Jessie stopped her by saying, "Juanita, I want to ask you a question."

The maid turned timidly toward her. "*Sí*, señorita?"

"You grew up in this valley, didn't you?"

"*Sí*. My father has always had a farm here."

"Then what happened tonight . . . you've seen it before, haven't you?"

Juanita's head bobbed up and down. "*Sí*, señorita. El Monte del Fuego has spoken many times."

"Always the same way? Or is it getting worse?"

Juanita frowned and hesitated, then finally said, "The noise, it is getting worse. Louder. And it comes more often. The sky is *muy rojo*. More red than it used to be."

"That's what I was afraid of," Jessie murmured.

Juanita laced her hands together anxiously. "It is said among my people that when the spirits of the mountain are displeased by the evil in the valley, they throw down fire and death on the good and evil alike. Do you think this is true, Señorita Starbuck?"

"I don't know, Juanita," Jessie said honestly, shaking her head. "I just don't know. . . ."

Angry shouts, followed closely by a gunshot, woke Ki. He came awake almost instantly, sitting up on the bunk, his muscles tensed for action. Even though all his senses were alert, for a split second he didn't know where he was.

124

Then he glanced around the inside of the crude little hut and remembered the Reverend Doctor Timothy Wayland and the young Mexican woman called Ana.

The noises that had roused him from his deep sleep came from outside. As Ki swung his legs off the bunk, stood up, and pulled his pants on, he heard a harsh voice demanding loudly, "Do not lie to me, dog! I saw the tracks. Where is the man you brought here?"

"I . . . I brought no one." That was Wayland. "I would not lie to you, Señor Perez."

Perez! Ki stiffened even more. The bandit chieftain was here, tracking him down. But why? Perez had gotten what he wanted: the train, Jessie, Lucifer.

Hadn't he?

"Very well," Perez said. "Perhaps you will sing a different song, gringo, once my men are through with your woman!"

Ki heard a female scream, shrill and full of terror. His jaw tightened. That was Ana.

He moved toward the flimsy door that was closed over the hut's entrance. The door was thin enough so that he could plainly hear the laughter of several men and the little gasps of horror from Ana that followed her scream. Ki heard cloth ripping, too.

His vest was draped over the back of one of the rough-hewn chairs. He picked it up and shrugged into it. He was already wearing one of Wayland's shirts, which had replaced the torn, dirty, and bloodstained one he'd had on when they brought him here the day before. His fingers dipped into the pockets of the vest, bringing a smile to his face as he touched the *shuriken* and the remaining throwing knife. He wouldn't have to face the *bandidos* completely unarmed, anyway. He would probably be badly outnumbered, but perhaps if he surrendered to Perez, the outlaw would leave Wayland and Ana alone.

125

Ki was becoming aware now of how painful and difficult it was for him to move. The rush of blood through his veins when the shouts and the gunshot woke him up had blocked some of the discomfort, but now it was coming back strong. He was covered with bruises from the fall into the arroyo the day before, and the bullet wounds in his arm and on his hip were throbbing as well.

But he could not give in to the pain. He had to reach inside himself, to the resources he had learned to tap while he was under the tutelage of the great samurai Hirata. His *sensei* had taught him that everything was within the grasp of he who would believe and take it. Ki closed his eyes, blocked from his mind for the moment the cries of Ana and the protests of Wayland, and drew several deep breaths into his body. He felt strength flowing out from the core of his being, assuaging the hurts, loosening stiff muscles, clearing his thoughts, his heart, and his brain. When he opened his eyes again, his expression was alert but calm, ready for anything.

He pushed the door of the hut open, stepped out into the morning sunlight, and called sharply, "Stop! Leave the woman alone!"

Instantly he spotted Lucardo Perez as the bandit leader turned toward him. Perez was on horseback. He had not come here alone, and his men—about a dozen of them, Ki saw—had dismounted so that they could shove Ana back and forth between them and snatch her clothes off. Ki caught a glimpse of her, nude and terrified, in their midst as the *bandidos* also whirled to face him. Guns leapt into the hands of several of them.

"No!" Perez called, gesturing curtly at his followers. "Do not shoot, amigos! I remember this one from Monterrey. He is a very brave man."

Ki made no response to the mocking compliment. He

stood motionless as Perez clucked to his horse and walked the animal toward him. A flick of Ki's eyes told him that Wayland was standing off to one side, his lantern-jawed face a confused mixture of anger, frustration, and fear.

Perez brought his mount to a halt about five feet in front of Ki and crossed his hands on the saddle horn as he leaned forward. "When I saw the tracks and figured out that this old man had rescued a survivor from the train, I had no idea it would be you, Chinaman. You are a warrior. You killed some of my men in Monterrey when they tried to take the horse of Don Arturo Hernandez."

Ki didn't bother correcting Perez about his ancestry or confirming the bandit's memory about what had happened in Monterrey. He faced Perez coolly and said, "You have no quarrel with Reverend Wayland or the girl. You should leave them alone. I am the one you are looking for."

Perez frowned. "The old man lied to me—Lucardo Perez! I cannot allow such a thing. And my men can always use another woman." He glared at Ki for a second, then went on. "But it is true that you are the reason I am here. If you tell me what I want to know, I will kill you quickly and leave the old man unharmed. The girl, however, comes with us."

That bargain was unacceptable to Ki, but he knew he had no leverage at the moment. The first thing he had to do was find out just what in blazes Perez thought he knew that was so important.

"What is it you wish to know?"

"You were on the train after it left the main route and took the old spur line. Can you tell me who took it and where they were going?"

Ki's first impulse was to gape at the man in disbelief. Instead, he kept his face carefully emotionless as he said, "Your men took the train."

Perez shook his head. "No. I tell you the truth, Chinaman. We planned to stop the train, *sí*. That devil horse will be mine if I have to chase him all the way to Baja California! But the barrier we placed on the tracks was a good five miles north of the old spur line. The train never reached us."

"Then who—" The surprised exclamation was out of Ki's mouth before he could restrain it.

Perez's eyes narrowed. "You do not know who stopped the train, do you, Chinaman?"

"It was your men," Ki said stubbornly, hoping his momentary slip hadn't bought him a quick bullet through the brain. "We saw them."

Perez shook his head and said, "Not my men. *Bandidos,* perhaps, but not those of Lucardo Perez." He sighed. "I think maybe you are not going to be so useful to me after all, Chinaman."

Quickly Wayland spoke up. "I can take you to where that spur line ends, Señor Perez. That's the only place the train could have gone."

Perez glowered at him. "I know this already, gringo fool! What I want to know is who did this to me. Who stole that black horse out from under the nose of Lucardo Perez?"

The wheels of Ki's brain were clicking over rapidly. He wanted to keep Perez talking, so he asked, "What did you find when you went down the rail line looking for the train?"

"A bunch of scared, huddled peons!" Perez replied contemptuously. "They thought we had come back to finish them off and did not want to believe me when I said that we had nothing to do with the attack on the train. I had to shoot a couple of them to convince them that I was telling the truth. Then they said that whoever took over the train left with it, heading up that old spur line into the mountains. We followed. But then I saw the tracks where someone had been thrown from the train into an arroyo and then brought here, so we came to find out what you knew." He added coldly, "I see now that we have wasted our time."

As Perez drew a holstered pistol, Wayland said, "What about my offer? I'll guide you, Señor Perez."

"We don't need no gringo guide," Perez sneered. "My amigos and me know these mountains better than you ever could, old man. We will go to where the mines used to be and pick up the trail there." He motioned to his men. "Mount up, and throw the girl onto one of the horses."

"No!" Wayland cried raggedly. "You can't take her!"

Ana screamed again and struggled futilely against the hard hands of the men who grabbed her and pulled her toward the horses.

Ki knew he was going to have to sell his life as dearly as possible and hope that Ana and Wayland could get away in the confusion. His fingers flickered into the pocket of his vest and closed on a *shuriken*. He would take Perez first. At least the bandit would die for his crimes.

Wayland leapt toward Ki as Perez brought up the pistol and cocked it hurriedly. "Stop!" the old man cried. "You mustn't—"

"Get out of the way!" Ki said desperately. The *shuriken* was in his hand, but he couldn't throw it while Wayland was between him and Perez.

Wayland flung his hands up and got in front of Perez just as the outlaw fired. The bullet bored into his chest and drove him backward into Ki. Ki tried to flip the *shuriken* underhand at Perez as he was falling backward, knocked off balance by the collision with Wayland, but the throw was off. The shining, deadly silver star flew past Perez's head, its only effect to make the bandit even more furious.

Perez fired again as Wayland and Ki went down. The bandit urged his horse forward and emptied his pistol into Wayland's body, placing all the shots in the old man's chest and making a bloody ruin of it. "Let the bullets do for both of you!" the *bandido* grated. At this range the heavy-caliber slugs would tear completely through Wayland's body and into Ki's. The bodies of both men jerked crazily under the impact of the bullets.

When his gun was empty, Perez drew a deep breath and glared down at the bodies. Wayland's eyes stared sightlessly at the bright blue morning sky, while Ki's eyes were closed and his face was obscured by blood. Perez looked over at his men as he started reloading his gun. Ana was mounted in front of one of the *bandidos,* nude and sobbing in grief as she stared wide-eyed at the corpses of Wayland and Ki.

Perez jerked a thumb at the bodies, and one of the men got down to come over and place a hand at the throat of each of them. After a moment, the bandit looked up and nodded to Perez. *"Muerto."*

"Bueno," Perez grunted. "We go now."

He rode away toward the old deserted mining camp where the spur line ended, and his men followed, bringing Ana with them.

Behind them, buzzards began to circle lazily in the sky.

★

Chapter 16

Jessie slept surprisingly soundly. Exhaustion had a way of doing that, she supposed as she woke up and stretched, enjoying the smoothness of the cool, clean sheets against her bare skin. There had been a nightgown for her to sleep in, but she had ignored it, preferring to slip nude into the bed.

She sat up, sighing as she ran her fingers through her tousled hair. Creature comforts were one thing, and a part of her couldn't help but enjoy them.

But Jessie could not forget that she and Silencio Ryan were still prisoners, and that Ki, her best friend in the world, was probably dead, along with everyone else on the train who had been slaughtered by the Corrales vaqueros.

She swung her legs out of the bed and stood up to go to the window with its iron grillwork, taking the top sheet with her to wrap around her. It was a beautiful morning, she saw, clear and bright. From this window, she could look up at the snowcapped peak of the Mountain of Fire. A wisp of something trailed away from the summit. Blowing snow? Jessie wondered. Or smoke from the volcano?

She and Ryan had to get out of here. She was no scientist, but from what Juanita had said about the tremors and the red glow in the sky when the mountain shook, it sounded to Jessie like an eruption was drawing ever closer. If the mountain ever blew its top off and sent a deadly wave of lava flowing down into the valley, it would wash away this hacienda like a sandcastle before a flood.

A key clattered in the lock of the door. Jessie swung around sharply as the heavy wooden door opened. Esteban Corrales stood there, a smile on his handsome face.

"Ah, you are awake already," he said. "*Buenos dias,* Jessica. And you are looking very lovely this morning, I might add."

Jessie was very aware of the fact that she was nude underneath the thin sheet wrapped around her. She nodded curtly to Corrales and said, "I need some clothes to wear. Juanita took my others away, and the gown I had on last night got torn." Her tone was scathing as she reminded him of what had happened.

Corrales didn't seem to take offense. "Of course," he said. "I shall have Juanita bring some things for you. Then, if you will do me the honor of joining me downstairs for breakfast . . ."

Jessie didn't see any way out of it. She nodded.

"And afterward," Corrales continued, "I will show you around my rancho. After all, since you will be living here, you should be familiar with your new home."

"All right," Jessie said. Let him think that she was going to behave herself, she thought. He would find out different soon enough.

At least she hoped with all her heart that would be the case.

Juanita brought her a pair of high black boots, some black pants that molded themselves sensuously to the curves of her thighs and hips, a white silk shirt, and a brown leather vest. The maid also had with her a beautiful red rose.

"Señor Corrales wants you to wear this in your hair, señorita," Juanita told her as she held out the rose when Jessie was finished dressing.

Jessie took the flower and pinned it in her hair above her right ear. Juanita clapped her hands together.

"The señorita is *muy bonita!*"

"Thanks," Jessie said. "I can't help but wish I was getting fixed up for somebody besides Corrales, though."

"I . . . I am sure you will come to care for him."

"Don't bet on it," Jessie told the young woman.

She left the room, Juanita trailing behind her. As Jessie started along the gallery that led to the broad staircase, another door opened and a man stepped out to bar her path. She stopped short and frowned in surprise at Lupe Corrales. The fat man was sweating, as usual. As he lifted a cloth to mop his face, he looked past Jessie and snapped a command in Spanish at Juanita. Jessie could follow enough of it to know that Lupe was telling the maid to leave them alone.

"Señor Esteban told me to escort Señorita Starbuck down to breakfast—" Juanita began.

"And I am telling you to do as I say," Lupe snapped. "*Vamanos!* I will see that Señorita Starbuck reaches the dining room."

Reluctantly, Juanita turned and went back along the gallery, disappearing through an archway with a last worried look over her shoulder at Jessie and Lupe. Jessie faced him squarely and said, "What do you want with me?"

"I . . . I wish to tell you, señorita, that none of this was my idea. I must do as Esteban says, of course, but if it was up to me, I would never have kidnapped you, nor stolen that horse, nor killed all those people at the train."

"You didn't protest very hard, though, did you, when

133

your brothers came up with this plan?" Jessie's voice was hard and cold. Maybe she was being too rough on Lupe, she thought fleetingly, but she wanted to know how sincere he was about his regrets.

Maybe if he really meant what he was saying, his feelings of guilt just might come in handy. . . .

"Truly I did not want these things to happen," the fat man said, almost pathetically eager to be believed. "But Esteban and Emiliano would not be denied. Esteban is so strong and accustomed to imposing his will on everyone, and Emiliano is a genius who cares nothing for people. All that matters to him are his books and his studies . . . and Esteban's approval, since it is Esteban's riches that pay for our life here."

"And you wouldn't want anything to interfere with that life, either, would you, Lupe?" Jessie prodded.

He shook his head. "I dare not oppose Esteban. He would . . . he would kill me."

"He's your brother!"

"It would not matter to him, if he thought I stood between him and something he wanted."

Jessie moved a step closer to him. "What do *you* want, Lupe?"

He swallowed hard, and for an instant she saw his eyes drop to the proud thrust of her breasts against the silk shirt. Quite clearly, an appetite for food was not the only appetite he possessed.

But his fear of his brother overwhelmed everything else, Jessie realized a moment later, to her disappointment. He said, "I cannot help you. I simply cannot, no matter what you . . . no matter what you offer me in return. So do not waste your time. I . . . I am sorry I bothered you. I will take you to Esteban now." He stepped aside and gestured for her to precede him.

Jessie sighed. For a moment, she had thought she'd glimpsed an opportunity to turn Lupe against his brothers. If the fat man had agreed to help her, she and Ryan would have been one step closer to getting out of this isolated, potentially deadly valley.

She walked quickly to the staircase, making Lupe hurry to keep up with her. On the way down the stairs, he kept repeating under his breath, "I am sorry, I am sorry . . ."

Corrales was waiting in the dining room, just as he had been the night before. He arched one eyebrow in surprise when he saw Lupe come into the room with Jessie. "What are you doing here?" he asked sharply. "You have already eaten."

"I know, Esteban," Lupe said quickly. "I just thought I would escort Señorita Starbuck down here to you."

"I told Juanita to do that." Corrales's voice was icy.

"I know, but she was suddenly taken ill," Lupe lied. "I was just trying to help."

"There are servants for that." Corrales turned his attention to Jessie, obviously forgetting about Lupe. "Please sit down," he told her as he gestured to the chair on his right. Lupe slunk out of the room as Jessie took her seat.

For breakfast, there were more platters of fruit, along with eggs, steak, and tortillas. Jessie's appetite was still healthy enough, so she ate well, although not too heartily. If the opportunity arose for her and Ryan to make a break for freedom, she didn't want to be sluggish from eating too much.

Corrales didn't mention what had happened on the terrace the night before, nor did he say anything about the ominous volcanic activity in the mountain. Jessie couldn't see the top of the mountain from where she was sitting, but she could look past Corrales and see some of the slope through the French doors. She wished she could peer right through those layers of rock and dirt and see what was going on inside the earth. Not that she would have really understood what she was seeing if that had been possible, she thought. But having such forces seething so close by, yet completely out of sight, made her nervous.

When they were finished eating, Corrales took her outside. Not through the French doors to the terrace this time, but rather out the front of the house and around the wall toward the area where the bunkhouse, corrals, and barns were located. She saw that Corrales had spared no expense in housing the horses that he raised here; the quarters for the men were more spartan and obviously slapped together. If the vaqueros resented such treatment, however, they gave no sign of it. Jessie figured that Corrales paid them well for their services. He would have to, when those services included holding up trains and murdering innocent people.

"You see now my pride and joy," Corrales said as he waved a hand toward a large corral where several colts scampered about. "At least for the time being. These are the offspring of El Rey and my best mares. In time they will be joined by the colts sired by Lucifer." He leaned on the fence, his face shaded by the flat-crowned hat he wore, and nodded in approval as he studied the colts. "Give me five years," he went on, "and I will produce colts the likes of which my country has never seen. They will be the fastest, most beautiful horses ever."

With such an obviously fine bloodline already in place to work with, and with the addition of Lucifer, Jessie had no doubt Corrales was right. But the price was so high, too high for any sane person to pay.

Lucifer came out of one of the barns into a large corral, led by Silencio Ryan. Jessie caught her breath at the sight of the big redhead. Ryan hadn't noticed her yet, which gave her a moment to study him unawares. He seemed to be all right, but he was moving a little stiffly. A result of the blow to the small of the back the day before, Jessie would have wagered. He had probably pissed blood when he got up that morning, she thought. There were no other horses in the corral with Lucifer, but two of Corrales's men came into the pen following Ryan and Lucifer, and they kept their hands on their guns. That was just in case Ryan tried anything, Jessie supposed.

"Ah, Lucifer!" Corrales exclaimed as he looked over and saw the big black stallion. "Let us go and see him."

He linked his arm with Jessie's and led her toward the other corral. Ryan was standing back while Lucifer trotted around the pen, stretching his legs. When he saw them coming, Ryan stiffened. Jessie felt a quick flush of shame. In these new clothes, with a rose in her hair, parading around on Corrales's arm, she wouldn't have blamed Ryan if he thought she had gone over to the enemy.

When he looked at her, though, Ryan's expression held nothing but solicitude, and his glance at Corrales was pure hate. He was smart enough, Jessie realized, to know that her cooperation was intended only to keep both of them alive.

"*Buenos dias,* Señor Ryan," Corrales said in greeting. "How is Lucifer this morning?"

"None the worse for wear, I reckon," Ryan answered dryly. "Wish I could say the same thing for me."

"You will not be mistreated as long as you cooperate," Corrales assured him. "I wish for you to teach my men how to handle Lucifer and help the horse become adjusted to them."

"Sure, but as soon as I do that, you won't have any more need of me, and I'll get a bullet in the back of the head."

"Nonsense. I do not forget those who help me."

None of them believed that. Jessie knew as well as Ryan did that as soon as he had outlived his usefulness, Corrales would have him killed. And Corrales had to know they were aware of that fact. It was all a game to the suave *hacendado*, Jessie realized. He didn't care if they believed him or not, as long as the game went on as planned.

Ryan walked purposefully toward the fence, ignoring the way the vaqueros tensed behind him. As they slipped their guns from leather, Corrales motioned for them to back off. Ryan came up to the fence and said, "Are you all right, Jessie?"

"I'm fine, Silencio," she told him. "What about you?"

"I'll live. And I'll get us out of this mess somehow."

"Ah, but there is no mess from which Señorita Starbuck needs rescuing, Señor Ryan," Corrales said. "This is her home now, and yours as well. The sooner you realize that, the happier we all will be."

"I won't be happy until you're bait for the *zopilotes,* Corrales," Ryan grated.

"Then I should have you shot right now, to save myself the trouble later," Corrales said coolly. Once again, his men started to lift their guns, and Jessie tensed.

Corrales shook his head and went on. "I will not do that, however, because I know that in the end, you will not risk the life of Señorita Starbuck, or that of Lucifer's. You are defeated, Señor Ryan. You are no longer a threat to me."

Ryan held his angry stare on Corrales for a moment longer, then dropped his eyes toward the ground inside the pen. Jessie felt a brief, irrational surge of disappointment until she realized that Ryan was just doing the same thing she was—trying not to push Corrales too far, too soon. She was sure she could still count on the big redhead when the time came.

"Come with me," Corrales told her as he turned away from Lucifer's pen. "We will go riding, and I will show you the rest of the ranch. I will even allow you to ride El Rey."

"Thank you," Jessie said. She wasn't going to waste an opportunity to ride the big, powerful roan. There was always a chance she might be mounted on El Rey when she left here for the final time, and she wanted to have an idea how the roan handled and whether or not it could outdistance any pursuit.

She glanced over her shoulder as she and Corrales went toward the other stables. Ryan had gone back to exercising Lucifer.

Stay alive, Jessie thought. *Stay alive, Silencio, and wait for a break.*

Chapter 17

Ki waited as long as he could before he moved. He opened his eyes a slit and watched through the film of blood over his face as the buzzards wheeling through the sky overhead dipped lower and lower.

It had been at least half an hour since Lucardo Perez and the rest of the *bandidos* had ridden off, Ki estimated. Even if Perez had been the least bit suspicious that he was still alive—and that was doubtful—anyone left behind to keep an eye on the bodies would have surely moved on by now. Nobody could lie there in the ever-growing heat and pretend to be dead for that long as ants and other insects swarmed over him.

Nobody except one man.

Ki was not sure how he had come to be still alive. By all rights, he should have been dead, killed by the bullets fired through Timothy Wayland's body and into his own.

Except that none of Perez's shots had penetrated all the way through Wayland's body for some reason. Ki was unharmed. The blood on him had come from Wayland's chest, splattering up and over the man's shoulder and into Ki's face as Perez pumped slug after slug into Wayland.

The idea had flashed into Ki's mind at that moment, and

he had acted on it instantly. He'd closed his eyes and let his mind slip into a sort of dream state, slowing his pulse and his breathing until both were almost imperceptible. If the *bandido* who had thrust his grimy fingers against Ki's throat had kept them there thirty seconds longer, he might have felt the faint stirring that signified Ki was still alive.

The desperate gamble had paid off, Ki knew now. He opened his eyes wider as one of the buzzards landed on Wayland's chest and dipped its ugly bald head to feast on the carnage there.

Ki waved an arm and yelled, and the *zopilote* took off with a surprised, angry squawk. The scavenger bird had been convinced that both of the men lying on the ground were dead, and if he could fool a buzzard, Ki thought, he had surely fooled Perez and the rest of the bandits.

As gently as he could, Ki pushed Wayland's body aside. He sat up, feeling the slight tremors of a delayed reaction going through him. A couple of deep breaths steadied him. He looked over at Wayland and saw something strange about the way the blood-drenched peasant shirt lay against the man's ruined chest. There was something else there, underneath the shirt. . . .

Carefully, Ki lifted the shirt and slid his hand under it. His fingers closed over a thick book, which would not have been very noticeable under the loose folds of the garment. Ki had certainly not noticed that Wayland was carrying it, and Perez hadn't, either.

The book, Ki realized, was a Christian Bible. Wayland had said that he had been a minister in the past, before the downfall that had led him to this Mexican wilderness. Obviously he had not severed all the connections with his past, because he had still been carrying this Bible. And while it had not protected him from evil, it had certainly saved Ki's life.

Because there were five bullet holes in it, one for each of the shots that Perez had fired.

The bandit leader's accuracy with his pistol had backfired on him, Ki thought grimly. The heavy slugs had penetrated the Bible and killed Wayland, but the thick volume had slowed down the bullets enough that they didn't have the force to tear on through Wayland's body and into Ki. If Perez had not grouped his shots so closely together, one of them would have surely missed the Bible and gone on through Wayland.

It was a mistake, Ki thought, that Lucardo Perez would live to regret.

Perez and his men had been on their way to the old abandoned mines at the end of the spur line, intending to pick up the trail of whoever had stolen the train at that point. That was the only starting point Ki had, as well. He intended to follow the *bandidos,* and sooner or later he would catch up to them. He hoped that when he did, he would also find Jessie and Ryan and Lucifer.

First, though, there were things he had to do here. He found an old spade in the hut and used it to scrape out a shallow grave in the hard, rocky ground. An old blanket had to serve as Wayland's burial shroud. Ki rolled the man in it after placing the Bible on Wayland's chest and crossing his hands over it. After Ki had lowered the body into the grave and replaced the dirt, he piled as many rocks as he could on top of it to form a cairn. Then, not knowing what sort of religious ritual the old man would have preferred— if any—Ki simply lifted his face to the sky and said aloud, "This was a good man. Let him be at peace."

With that done, Ki turned his attention to the future. He didn't know how long this pursuit he was setting out on would be, so he packed a bundle of food from the meager supplies in the hut and filled a waterskin at a nearby spring.

It was not difficult to find the tracks left by the horses of the *bandidos*. Without looking back at the jacal, Ki began following them, moving at a ground-eating trot that he could keep up all day under normal conditions. With his wounds, he knew he would have to be careful not to push himself too hard. He wouldn't be any good to Jessie if he was too exhausted to fight when he caught up to the bandits.

Jessie wasn't his only consideration, either. Perez and his men had taken Ana with them. Ki tried hard not to think too much about the terror she must be experiencing right now. He hoped he could free her before she had to endure too much torment at the hands of the gang.

The sun rose higher in the sky and became hotter and hotter. A fine sheen of sweat appeared on Ki's features as he relentlessly followed the trail left by Perez. At midday he stopped, ate one of the tortillas he had brought from the hut, and took a small sip of water. That was enough. He trotted on.

Early in the afternoon, he reached the broad canyon in the foothills where the spur line ended. The train sat there, empty, abandoned. Ki stopped and crouched behind a bush, watching to make sure no one was nearby before he approached the train. The mouths of the abandoned mines yawned darkly on the hillsides around him.

When he was convinced that it was safe, he moved down to the tracks of the spur line and along them to the train itself. Quickly he looked through the cars. They had been looted—seat cushions slashed, the seats themselves broken, everything of the least value stripped from them. Ki had hoped to find some guns. Even though he didn't like firearms, under the circumstances he wouldn't have minded having something to make the odds against him a bit less overpowering. It was a futile hope, though. No weapons of any kind had been left behind.

He remembered the words of Hirata. A man's greatest weapons are his mind and his heart, the samurai had said. Ki still had those two things, so he was well armed indeed, he told himself.

A check of the locomotive's engine told him it was cold, the fire in the box dead since the day before. Ki leapt down from the cab and studied the tracks left on the hard ground alongside the rails. There were more of them now. He was seeing the tracks left not only by Perez's gang, he realized, but also those of the men who had taken over the train. All of them had set off on horseback toward one of the smaller canyons that branched off to the side of the main one.

Ki followed as well. There was nothing else he could do.

Corrales's ranch was impressive, Jessie had to admit that. It was nothing like her own vast Circle Star spread back in Texas, of course, but still impressive. Herds of horses and cattle grazed throughout the valley, except for the areas that were cultivated to provide produce for the ranch. Jessie wasn't surprised that the hacienda had made Corrales a rich man.

But riches obviously weren't enough for him; otherwise he wouldn't steal horses and kidnap people. To Esteban Corrales, power was even more important than money. And power meant letting nothing stand in the way of anything he wanted, not even the lives of innocent people.

From time to time as they rode around the ranch, Jessie glanced at the snowcapped peak at the head of the valley. Wisps of steam still rose from it. That meant it was growing hotter up there, and she wondered if the snow on the slopes had begun to melt. There had been no more tremors, but Jessie still found her gaze drawn anxiously to the peak, as if some instinct deep inside her sensed that danger lay there just under the surface.

Corrales didn't seem worried at all, but that came as no surprise. The man was so arrogant, he probably thought that no volcano would dare to erupt while he was around. He was in for a surprise one of these days, Jessie thought.

And she hoped that when it came, it wouldn't kill everyone else in the valley.

When they returned to the house for lunch, Lupe and Emiliano joined them for the meal, the first one Corrales's brothers had shared with them since Jessie had been there. She caught Lupe staring at her several times, and she smiled at him, embarrassing him but pleasing him at the same time. She hadn't completely given up hope of getting some help from the fat man, so she considered the smile well spent.

Corrales must have noticed Lupe looking at her, too, because when the meal was over he said sharply, "Jessica and I would be alone now."

Emiliano made no protest as he got up and headed for his own rooms on the second floor. Jessie figured he was anxious to get back to his "studies," whatever they were. He wasn't a very sociable type to start with. Lupe, however, got to his feet and began nervously, "If there is anything I can do—"

"Nothing," Corrales snapped. "Leave us now, Lupe."

The man nodded and muttered, *"Sí, sí,"* and shuffled out of the dining room.

Corrales rested his elbows on the table and laced his fingers together. "What would you like to do this afternoon, *querida?*" he asked.

"I'm . . . a little tired from the ride," Jessie said. "I'd like to rest for a while."

"An excellent idea. Shall I . . . accompany you to your room?"

"I said I'd like to rest," Jessie repeated pointedly.

Corrales inclined his head in acknowledgment and said, "Very well. But tonight . . ." He drew a deep breath. "Tonight will be, as you Americans say, a different story."

Meaning that he would no longer allow her to refuse his advances, Jessie figured. She had been expecting as much. But she merely murmured, "The night is always different from the day," and let him draw his own conclusions.

Evidently he liked the ones he drew, because he smiled at her, then clapped his hands and called, "Juanita!"

The maid appeared, as soft-spoken and diffident as ever. "*Sí*, Señor Esteban?"

"Escort Señorita Starbuck back to her room."

Jessie said, "I can find my own way by now."

"I am certain you can," Corrales said. "But Juanita will go with you in case you need anything."

And to keep an eye on her, Jessie thought. That was all right. She hadn't expected anything else. Corrales wasn't about to just give her free run of the place, not yet. And maybe never.

When they reached the bedroom, Juanita asked, "Is there anything I can do for you, señorita?"

Jessie shook her head. "I'm going to lie down for a while."

"*Sí*. I will be back later." Juanita started toward the door, then stopped and looked back at Jessie. She asked hesitantly, "Now that you have spent more time with Don Esteban, do you . . . do you feel differently about him?"

"Are you going to go back downstairs and tell him whatever I say?" Jessie asked coolly.

Juanita shook her head emphatically. "No, señorita. This thing I ask, it is between only you and me."

For some reason, Jessie believed the young woman. She said quietly, "No, Juanita. My feelings haven't changed.

146

And they won't as long as my friend Señor Ryan and I are being held prisoner here."

"I . . . I think that you are good." Juanita took a deep breath and plunged ahead. "I think Don Esteban should let you go."

"If I thought it would do any good, I'd tell you to tell him that." An idea occurred to Jessie, and she looked at the other woman shrewdly. "You think if I wasn't here, Corrales might decide to take you back as his woman?"

Juanita shook her head without hesitation, but Jessie thought she saw a flash of something in the maid's eyes. That was it, Jessie thought. Juanita had not completely given up on the idea that she would one day win back the affections of Corrales. Jessie had a feeling the girl was doomed to disappointment, though. Corrales had no deep feelings for anyone. He was toying with all of them.

Juanita ducked out before Jessie could press her any further on the issue. The key clattered firmly in the lock as Juanita twisted it.

Jessie sighed and took the rose out of her hair, laying the flower on the dressing table. She slipped out of the vest and her boots, then lay down on the bed. What she had told Corrales about being tired wasn't just a lie to get away from him; she really was still weary from everything that had happened. She meant to just rest for a while, but without being aware of when it happened, she drifted off to sleep instead.

Something roused her from slumber, and as Jessie blinked her eyes open and lifted her head from the soft pillow, she tried to figure out how much time had passed. Sunshine still came through the window, so it wasn't evening yet. The house was quiet, and as she listened, she didn't even hear any noise coming from outside. The entire ranch seemed to be dozing.

Of course, she told herself. It was still siesta time.

And in the silence, she could hear the faint noise at the door that much better.

That quiet rasp of metal against metal must have been what woke her, she thought as she sat up and turned toward the door. Someone was turning the key in the lock, but slowly and carefully, trying not to make much noise.

Corrales, coming up here to insist on finally having his way with her? Juanita, slipping back into the room for some unknown reason? Or someone else?

Jessie glanced around, looking instinctively for some sort of weapon. There was nothing. She had been tutored in the martial arts for years by Ki, however, and if she were forced to fight barehanded, she was confident she could give a good account of herself.

The lock finally clicked open, and the door began to swing slowly toward her. Jessie tensed, ready to spring up off the bed and dart into action if necessary.

A bulky shape stepped into the room, closed the door softly, then turned to face Jessie. Lupe Corrales gasped as he saw that she was not only awake but watching him with suspicion. He looked pale and frightened.

"What do you want?" Jessie hissed.

"Please, señorita, please." Lupe made pushing motions with his hands. "Do not be alarmed." He swallowed hard. "I . . . I have come to help you."

Well, it was damned well about time, Jessie thought. Time for *somebody* to stand up to Esteban Corrales.

"Come in," she said as she stood up. "We'll talk about it."

★

Chapter 18

Lupe was so nervous Jessie was afraid he was going to collapse in a puddle of sweat on the floor. She had him sit down in one of the high-backed chairs in the room and then sat down on the bed facing him.

"Are you sure about this, Lupe?" she asked. "You're not afraid of your brother?"

"Of *course* I am afraid of Esteban!" he replied. "But . . . but he must not be allowed to harm you or Señor Ryan. This is not the first time he has stolen things . . . he was a thief before we ever came to this valley . . . but to have all those people on the train killed—!" A shudder ran through his corpulent body. "I fear that he has lost his mind. He must be stopped before he does something even more horrible."

Jessie wasn't sure what could be worse than the slaughter carried out when the train was taken over, but she didn't press Lupe on that point. Instead she asked, "How do you think you can help us?"

Lupe leaned forward in his chair. "I am no genius like Emiliano, but I . . . I had an idea. Tonight I will take a bottle of tequila to the men guarding your friend. I will tell them it is a present. Inside it I will put powders to make them sleep, and after they are unconscious, I can free Señor Ryan and give him a gun."

Jessie nodded slowly and said, "That might work if you're careful. What about me?"

"I will see to it that your door is unlocked. But you must slip out on your own and make your way to the stables. I will tell Señor Ryan to go there, too. You can take horses and ride away from here before Esteban even knows you are gone."

"It'll be dangerous," Jessie pointed out.

"*Sí*. But what is not without danger in life?"

"And after we've escaped, your brother will figure out that you had something to do with it. He'll know you must have drugged the liquor you plan to give to Silencio's guards."

Lupe frowned. "*Sí*, that is a problem."

It was more than that, Jessie thought. It was a major sticking point in an already half-baked plan. Unfortunately she hadn't come up with a better one.

Suddenly Lupe's expression of concern vanished. His round face lit up. "I know!" he said. "I will come with you and Señor Ryan."

"What?"

"I no longer wish to stay here anyway. True, my brothers are here, but Emiliano is as cold as the snow on top of the mountain, and Esteban is crazy! Besides, I fear that mountain. It rumbles and spits fire, and I know that one day soon it will explode and kill us all." He stood up and began to pace back and forth as the idea gripped him. "Yes! Yes, I must leave and never come back. Then Esteban cannot harm me."

Well, it *might* work, Jessie thought. If they caught every break and nothing went wrong. If something did, they were probably all dead.

Which was how they were likely going to wind up anyway, she added grimly to herself. Unless some better opportunity presented itself between now and tonight, she decided, Lupe's plan was worth trying.

She nodded to him. "We'll do it," she said. "Just don't get scared and back out on us."

He shook his head vehemently. "Oh, no, señorita, I would not do that. You can trust me."

Jessie hoped so—for his sake. Because if he intended to double-cross her and Ryan, she would make sure of one thing no matter what else happened.

Lupe Corrales would die.

Ki crouched motionless amid the cluster of rocks. He made no sound. The voices from below came clearly enough to his ears so that he was able to make out most of the words.

". . . will wait until nightfall," Perez was saying. "Then we will attack."

One of the other *bandidos* said worriedly, "Esteban Corrales has many men working for him, Lucardo. Many more than there are of us."

Ki peered carefully around a rock and saw Perez thump a fist against his chest. "*Mi amigos,* each of you are worth ten of those vaqueros! Corrales's men are dogs, while we, muchachos, are wolves!"

There might be something to what Perez was saying, Ki thought. But from what he had seen of Corrales's men when they took over the train, those vaqueros could be every bit as cold-blooded and murderous as the real *bandidos*.

It had come as something of a shock to Ki a few minutes earlier when he first began eavesdropping on Perez's gang and discovered that the rancho in the valley below them belonged to Esteban Corrales. Ki had not liked Corrales when he met the man back in Monterrey, but he would not have thought that Corrales was brazen enough—or ruthless enough—to have pulled off something like the train takeover.

The proof was undeniable, however. The tracks Perez and his men had followed from the end of the spur line had led straight to this beautiful, isolated valley and the hacienda located there. From his hiding place, Ki could see the huge house built on the lower slopes of the mountain at the far end of the valley.

It was late afternoon. Ki had been trailing Perez and the *bandidos* for several hours, moving at the steady trot that had eaten up the ground surprisingly fast. In this rough terrain, it was possible for a man to run faster than a horse could walk, so Ki had been able to close the gap between himself and Perez's gang. Luckily, his keen ears had caught the faint clinking of harness and spurs up ahead in time for him to slow down and proceed cautiously. He had made his way through a jumble of boulders on the crest of a hill until he was some thirty feet above the broad, pine-dotted shelf where Perez and the other bandits had come to a halt to plan their strategy.

Within a few minutes, Ki had realized from the conversation among the *bandidos* that the ranch in the valley belonged to Esteban Corrales. Perez knew that, and evidently in the past he had given Corrales a wide berth, choosing not to raid this ranch as he had smaller haciendas. Ki remembered Wayland saying much the same thing about the bandit leader.

In the long run, it didn't matter to Ki who was responsible for the atrocity on the train. He intended to see whoever it was dead. He had thought that was Perez, but now that it was obvious Corrales was behind the attack, that was all right, too.

Ki just hoped that Jessie, Ryan, and Lucifer were still all right. If anything had happened to them, especially Jessie—

He shoved that thought out of his mind. He had other problems at the moment.

Like what to do about Ana.

He couldn't see her from where he was, but he knew she was down there somewhere. He could hear her sobbing. The sound tore at him, made him want to rush down there to protect her. Such a move would probably just get both of them killed, however, so he forced himself to be patient. None of the *bandidos* seemed to be molesting her at the moment. Maybe they would wait until after their raid on the Corrales ranch to do that. If they left her behind when they went to attack the hacienda, even if there were a couple of guards with her, Ki knew he would have little trouble freeing her. Then he could get down into the valley and use Perez's raid on the place as a distraction that would enable him to find Jessie, Ryan, and Lucifer and get them away from there.

Yes, that was the way it would be—in a perfect world.

This world, unfortunately, had never been perfect, Ki realized. And it was unlikely that it ever would be.

Because down below, Perez turned and barked at one of his men, "Bring the girl!"

Ki stiffened. Would he be able to stand by and do nothing while Perez and his men raped Ana? Or was that what they even had in mind? As one of the *bandidos* dragged Ana into view, holding her by the arm, Ki saw that someone had given her a woven serape. The garment had probably been colorful at one time, but now time and dirt had turned it an ugly shade of gray-brown. It was probably full of fleas, too. But Ana clutched it tightly about her, and Ki knew that it was better than being naked in the middle of a band of cutthroats and marauders.

Perez leered at Ana and jerked a thumb toward the valley. "You know this place, eh?" he asked.

From where he was hidden, Ki couldn't see Ana's face, but he saw the shudder that went through her. She said something, but her face was downcast and Ki couldn't understand her. Perez laughed at whatever it was she had said.

"*Sí*, that is El Monte del Fuego," he said. "Maybe you like it if we take you up there and throw you in, eh?"

Ana let out a low moan and fell to her knees. She caught hold of one of Perez's legs and clutched it desperately as she exclaimed, "Aaiii, no, señor! Anything but that!"

"Then you remember to please me and my men when we come back tonight, or that is where you will wind up, girl!" Perez roared at her, then threw back his head and let out a bellow of laughter. His men joined in his amusement.

Ki felt a surge of cold hatred. Perez and the other *bandidos* enjoyed terrifying a young, defenseless woman. They would feel differently if they were the ones being threatened. At that moment, Ki would have cheerfully shoved every one of them into the volcano.

He lifted his eyes to the peak at the head of the valley. So that was the Mountain of Fire, he thought. He remembered the tremor that had shaken Wayland's hut the night before. That disturbance must have been a lot stronger here in the valley. He hoped that if Jessie had been down there she hadn't been too frightened. Of course, he reminded himself, it took quite a bit to scare Jessica Starbuck.

Perez shoved Ana away from his leg with a curse and barked orders to a couple of his men. One of them grabbed her wrists, pulled them behind her, and tied them together. Then he dragged her over out of sight again and evidently shoved her down, because Ki heard her cry out. The bandit strode away, looking satisfied with himself.

Ki breathed a tiny sigh of relief. From the way Ana had been tied up, he guessed that they planned to leave her alone for the time being. He glanced at the sky; it would be dark soon, as nightfall descended with the suddenness it always did in this part of the world. As soon as it was good and dark, Perez and his men would start down into the valley to attack the Corrales ranch.

Then Ki would make his move, too. . . .

To one whose mind had not been trained in the discipline of the samurai, waiting was probably one of the most difficult things to do. Ki was able to find a secluded spot among the boulders, completely out of the view of the bandits, and sink down cross-legged to rest. He had covered many miles on foot this day, leaving his feet sore and his legs aching. The wounds on his hip and in his arm were throbbing, too. But he pushed all of the pain from his mind and concentrated instead on the feel of the soft wind on his face, the color of the last slanting red rays of the sun, the beautiful symmetry of a bird's wings as it glided by high above the valley, the sweet yet sharp tang of the pines. His senses were full, and he was content. He rested.

Yet he was well aware when darkness sank down from the heavens like paint sliding down a wall, and he heard the faint noises of Perez's men moving around as they prepared to depart on their murderous mission. Ki uncurled from the position he had assumed and walked silently among the rocks until he could look down at the bandit camp once more.

The *bandidos* were mounting up. Ki looked for Ana but couldn't see her. He saw, however, that one man was staying behind. That man stood near the edge of the shelf with his thumbs hooked in his crossed gunbelts.

Perez said in a loud voice, "Remember, that big black

horse is mine! Nothing must happen to it."

"What about Esteban Corrales?" one of the other men asked. "Do you want the honor of killing him yourself, *jefe?*"

Perez hawked up a gobbet of spittle and splattered it on the rocky ground beside his horse. "What honor is there in shooting down a craven cur?" he demanded. "Any of us can do it. All I demand is that Corrales and his brothers and all of their men die. I want no one left alive!"

Ki wondered if that also applied to Jessie and Ryan. Of course, Perez didn't know they were down there. For that matter, Ki himself couldn't be sure of that. But every instinct in his body told him that Jessie was there. They had been together for so long, through so many dangerous times, that he could sense her very presence.

Perez and the other men moved off down the slope of the hill toward the valley, leaving the guard behind. The man still stood at the edge of the shelf, watching the others depart. Ki could make him out in the feeble, silvery illumination from the stars and the thin sliver of moon that was rising to the east. Carefully, Ki moved out of the boulders and toward the clearing where the bandits had stopped and where Ana was still being held prisoner. He moved slowly, so that Perez and the others would have plenty of time to get out of earshot before he struck.

He froze as the guard turned and came toward him. Actually, the man was walking toward Ana, of course, but that also brought him closer to Ki. He called out softly to Ana, the words in Spanish. Ki understood enough of them to know that the guard was making a filthy suggestion about how they could pass the time until Perez returned. Ana said nothing in reply, but Ki was close enough now that he could hear her harsh, frightened breathing.

He wanted to reassure her somehow, let her know that

the *bandido* would never have the chance to carry out his crude proposal. Within minutes, the man would be dead. But to make any sort of noise now would tip his hand, Ki knew, and give the guard the opportunity to cry out or get a shot off. That would alert Perez that something was wrong up here.

The bandit was nothing more than a dark shape now, a shadow among shadows. Ki's eyes could still track him, though, as the man moved closer and then turned to face away from him. There was about an eight-foot drop to the flat shelf where Ana and the *bandido* were. Ki slipped his throwing knife from one of the pockets of his vest and gripped it tightly. The little blade was more suited for other things than close-in fighting, but for tonight it would have to do.

Stealthily, he moved a little closer, gauged the position of the bandit as best he could, then launched himself with a sudden flicker of motion in the darkness. Ki's left arm went around the neck of the guard from behind, squeezing tight to cut off the man's air and prevent any outcry. As the man struggled wildly against the unexpected attack out of the night and slapped at the butts of his pistols, Ki jerked up with the arm around his neck, lifting the bandit's chin and drawing tight the flesh of his throat.

Hot blood spurted over Ki's right hand as he drove the throwing knife into the man's throat and ripped it to the side. The man's arms and legs flapped wildly in a grotesque dance of death. A harsh rattling sound came from his now-open windpipe, but it wasn't loud enough to carry any distance.

The struggle lasted only a few seconds as blood continued to pump out over Ki's hand. It spurted like a fountain when he tore the blade free. The guard sagged against him, so much deadweight now. This part of the fight was over, and Ki could free Ana at last.

He was about to turn toward her when he felt the cold ring of metal press against the back of his neck and heard a hoarse, guttural curse in Spanish. At that instant, he realized what a terrible mistake he had made. He must have been more tired than he had thought.

There had been *two* guards left behind.

And one of them was about to blow his head off.

★

Chapter 19

The bandit had the drop on Ki, but the man couldn't resist a moment of gloating. As he dug the barrel of the pistol into the back of Ki's neck, he grated, "I kill you for what you have done, *bastardo!*"

"No!" Ana cried. Her hands were tied, but she awkwardly pushed herself onto her knees and dove toward the back of the man's legs.

Ki moved at the same instant, not sure what Ana was doing but knowing that this would be his only chance to avoid certain death. He sprang to the side, away from the gun, and whirled around in time to see Ana crash into the back of the bandit's knees and knock him forward. The *bandido* struggled to catch his balance and half turned to slash at Ana's head with the barrel of his gun.

Ki bent at the waist, his right leg lifting and then snapping out in a kick that slammed into the side of the gunman. The *bandido* was thrown off his feet. Ki was moving again before the man had even thumped heavily onto the ground. Ki lashed out, bringing both hands down in the deadly side-hand blows to the man's neck. The man twitched and stiffened and dropped his gun, and Ki was able to drive his right hand forward in a stiff-fingered thrust just under

159

the man's heart. The *bandido* gasped, his eyes bulging in pain and horror as the blow caused his heart to explode. He sagged back on the ground in death.

Ana was crying, ragged sobs that shook her body. Ki whirled toward her, uncertain whether or not the bandit had struck her with his gun. She seemed unharmed, though, as he gathered her in his arms and held her tightly to him.

"There now," Ki said softly as he stroked her hair and patted her back, feeling her trembling against him. "Hush, little one. It is all right now."

"K-Ki?" she asked in amazement. "It . . . it is you?"

"I am here," he confirmed.

"But . . . but you were dead!"

"The *bandidos* thought I was, but as you can see, I am not."

"Does that mean Señor Timothy is . . . is alive, too?"

Ki shook his head sadly. "I am sorry, Ana. Reverend Wayland is dead. I buried him before I started after Perez and his men."

That prompted some more crying. Ki held her while she sobbed, but his impatience was growing. He had to get down there into the valley while he still had a chance, before Perez and the other *bandidos* attacked the Corrales ranch.

He untied Ana's hands and had her sit down with her back against the bluff that bordered the shelf, where she had been before when he couldn't see her. The man whose throat he had cut had carried two pistols. Ki took the pair of cartridge belts and strapped them on, checking the revolvers to make sure they slid easily in their holsters. Then he scooped up the pistol the other man had dropped and pressed it into Ana's hands.

"I will come back for you," he promised, "but now I must leave. If Perez or any of his men come back, use this pistol to protect yourself. You can shoot, can't you?"

Her head jerked in a nod. "Señor Timothy taught me."

"Good. I'll be back as quickly as I can."

"I . . . I have to stay here with those . . . dead men?"

"Sorry. I forgot." Ki went to the corpses, lifted them one at a time, and heaved them over the edge of the shelf. They rolled down the slope and out of sight in the thick trees.

That seemed to make Ana feel a little better. She took a deep breath and used the back of her hand to wipe the tears from her face. "I am lucky," she said. "They did not harm me while they were chasing those other men. They were waiting until after they were finished tonight."

"I know," Ki nodded. "And now none of them will ever bother you."

"This you swear?"

"I swear," he said, hoping he could keep that pledge.

In the meantime, however, Perez's men were drawing closer to the hacienda with every passing moment, and Ki had already delayed long enough. He bent over, pressed his lips to the top of Ana's head in a quick kiss, then loped off the shelf and headed down the slope.

So far, no gunfire had broken out in the valley.

But it was just a matter of time, Ki thought. Just a matter of time. . . .

It was time, Jessie told herself.

Night had fallen, but she had not yet been summoned to the dining room to share the evening meal with Corrales. A few minutes earlier, footsteps had passed by in the corridor outside her door, and she had heard them pause for a second. The lock had clicked, and then the footsteps moved on.

Lupe had twisted the key in the lock, she knew, unlocking the door but leaving the key in it so that anyone else who passed by would think everything was normal. Jessie had waited for several minutes, giving Lupe enough time to get well away from the upstairs bedrooms. He was probably on his way outside now. Lupe would give the drugged liquor to Ryan's guards and free him when the vaqueros passed out. . . .

If everything went according to plan, that is. As Jessie began easing the door of her room open, she thought about all the things that could go wrong with this scheme. Everything had to be perfect—or they would all die.

She opened the door just wide enough for her to be able to peer down the hallway toward the stairs. No one was in sight. She listened intently and didn't hear anyone else moving around on this floor. She edged the door back a little more and ventured a look in the other direction even though that required sticking her head out farther.

No one there. Good.

Jessie was still wearing the clothes she had worn earlier in the day. They were comfortable enough to let her move freely. She had put the boots and the vest on again, but had left the rose on the dressing table. Tonight's activities weren't going to require any adornment. She would have gladly traded the rose for a revolver and a beltful of cartridges, had that been possible.

As it was, she was armed only with her skills, and that would have to be enough.

She wished she were more familiar with the layout of the house. Lupe had warned her not to go down the main stairway; there was another, smaller staircase at the rear of the house, he had told her. But if she had any trouble finding it, that could cause a dangerous delay.

Cat-footing along the gallery required only a moment. When Jessie reached the end of it, she saw that the corridor turned and ran toward the rear of the house. That was where she needed to go. She started along the hallway, past some closed doors.

One of them opened.

Jessie froze. There were no hiding places in this bare corridor. All she could do was stand there as Emiliano Corrales stepped out through the open doorway and then turned toward her. He stopped short, the deep-set eyes in his gaunt face widening in surprise as he saw her. His thin-lipped mouth opened, and she knew he was about to yell for his brother Esteban.

She struck, lunging toward him and driving the heel of her hand up underneath his chin, the way Ki had taught her.

The blow clicked Emiliano's teeth together and stifled any outcry for the moment. His head snapped back under the impact. Jessie barreled into him, driving him against the wall. His head struck the plaster with a hollow thump.

Emiliano's eyes rolled up in their sockets, and he sagged against Jessie. He was out cold, she realized as she caught him. Looping her arms around his thin chest, she dragged him back through the door from which he had emerged, into a room filled with books and a long table on which rested several glass beakers full of some noxious-looking liquid. Some sort of chemical experiment he was carrying out, Jessie decided.

He could finish it later, after she and Ryan were long gone from this valley.

Moving quickly, Jessie used Emiliano's belt to lash his ankles together, then tied his hands behind him with some cord she found in a large cabinet, with other supplies he no doubt used in his studies. She picked up a rag from the worktable and stuffed it into his mouth, then tied it in place with more of the cord. When he came to, he wouldn't be able to work himself loose or raise any sort of alarm for a long time. By then, she and Ryan would have either escaped—or lost their lives in the process.

She went back to the door of Emiliano's room and stepped into the hall, then stopped in her tracks as she almost ran into Juanita.

The maid gasped in shock, and Jessie moved quickly. Her hand shot out and clapped itself over Juanita's mouth. With her other hand, Jessie grabbed the young woman's arm and held it tightly. She leaned close to Juanita and hissed, "Please don't cry out. I don't want to hurt you."

Her eyes wide and frightened, Juanita managed to nod. Jessie took her hand away from her mouth, but kept her grip on Juanita's arm.

"Oh, Señorita Starbuck, what are you doing here?" Juanita whispered. "You are supposed to be in your room! Don Esteban sent me for to bring you down to the dining room."

"I won't be dining with Don Esteban tonight—or any other night," Jessie told her. "I'm getting out of here, Juanita, and I'm not going to let anything—or anyone—stop me. Not even you."

"Sí, I understand. But I'm afraid you will be hurt—"

"I'd rather die than live here as that madman's prisoner," Jessie said quietly.

Juanita looked at her sorrowfully for a moment, then sighed. "Sí. I know you are right. But I will miss you, señorita. I . . . I have grown fond of you, even in so short a time."

And speaking of short times, Jessie thought, she was running out of hers. She had to get the hell out of there. She looked intently at the maid and asked, "Can I trust you, Juanita?"

"Sí, señorita."

"Then I want you to go downstairs and tell Corrales that

164

I'm not feeling well. Tell him I'm too sick to have dinner with him. He probably won't believe that, but at least it'll buy me a few minutes."

"All right," Juanita agreed. "This thing I can do. But what are you going to do, señorita?"

"It's better that you don't know."

Juanita nodded again in understanding. Jessie let go of her arm and started to turn away, but Juanita put out a hand to stop her.

"Señorita . . . *vaya con Dios.*"

"*Gracias,* Juanita. And the same to you."

With that, Jessie hurried away down the corridor, heading toward the rear of the big house once again.

She spotted the narrow staircase a moment later. A glance over her shoulder told her that the hallway was empty. Juanita had already gone back downstairs to make her excuses to Corrales. He would think that Jessie was merely stalling and being stubborn, but he would probably wait a few minutes before coming upstairs himself and demanding to see her. By that time, Jessie intended to be out of the house and heading for her rendezvous with Ryan and Lupe.

She hoped they were ready to put this valley behind them for good.

"Drink up, *muchachos,* drink up. My brother wishes to reward you for your faithful service."

Silencio Ryan ran the brush over Lucifer's glossy black hide as he listened to Lupe Corrales urging the guards to polish off the bottle of tequila he had brought to them a few minutes earlier. Lupe had found them in the big barn where Lucifer was kept. The fat man had given Ryan a disdainful glance, then handed over the bottle of liquor he was carrying. It was a gift from Corrales, according to

Lupe. That didn't seem much like Corrales to Ryan, but he didn't know the rancher that well.

Just well enough to hate and despise him, in fact. . . .

Ryan had spent nearly all his time in captivity with Lucifer. It helped somehow to be near the big horse and know that the two of them were in this together. And of course there was Jessie. Ryan knew she hadn't betrayed him. She was just playing along with that bastard Corrales, waiting for the right moment to make a move against him. Ryan could wait, too. Just not too long, he hoped.

The two vaqueros who had been given the task of guarding him were sitting on short stools in the big aisle that ran down the center of the stable. Later, they would march him at gunpoint back to the big building that served as a barracks for the vaqueros. A narrow cot had been set up inside a tiny storage room with no windows and only one door. That was Ryan's prison cell whenever he wasn't here working with Lucifer. The one night he had spent on the cot so far had been miserable, since it was too short and narrow for him to sleep comfortably on it.

He looked over his shoulder and saw that there was only a swallow left in the bottle held by one of the guards. He said, "Hey, I could use a swig of that myself if you're not going to finish it off."

Lupe swung toward him angrily. "This tequila is not for the likes of you, dog! It is for these men—good, true, loyal men."

The vaquero holding the bottle gave Ryan an ugly grin, then lifted the bottle to his lips and drained it, his throat working as he swallowed the last of the tequila. He flung the empty bottle at Ryan, making him duck. The bottle shattered against the outer wall of Lucifer's stall. The horse snorted angrily at the unexpected sound.

Both vaqueros thought that was as funny as all get-out.

They slapped each other on the back and swayed back and forth and hooted. Then one of them swayed a little harder and harder still until he suddenly plunged off the stool and sprawled facedown on the dirt floor of the stable.

The other vaquero frowned at his *compadre* in surprise, then lifted startled eyes toward Lupe, who was beginning to look extremely nervous. The vaquero started to claw at the butt of his gun.

Then he slid off the stool and crumpled to the ground next to the other man.

"What the hell!" Ryan exclaimed.

Lupe swung hurriedly toward him. "Please, señor, there is no time! I have come to help you. It was my great good fortune that you were already here in the stable." He came toward Ryan, fumbling for something underneath his coat. He brought out a pistol.

Ryan tensed and clenched his fists, ready to leap forward and smash them into Lupe's fat face if the man tried to point the gun toward him. But instead, Lupe thrust the gun at him butt-first, saying, "Here, take this, señor. I do not know how to use it."

A savage grin stretched across Ryan's craggy features as he closed his fingers around the smooth wooden grips of the revolver. "Well, *I* sure as hell do. Is this on the level, hombre?"

"I swear I have come to help you escape. I, too, am leaving this valley. I want to get far away from my brother Esteban."

"Not a bad idea. But what about Jessie?"

"She should be here at any moment. I saw to it that the door of her room was unlocked before I came out here in search of you and your guards."

Ryan grunted in satisfaction and glanced toward the vaqueros, neither of whom had moved since slumping to

167

the ground. "I reckon you must have drugged that booze you brought to them."

"*Es verdad,*" Lupe agreed.

A footstep sounded suddenly at the entrance of the barn. The big double doors swung open. Ryan turned toward them, expecting to see Jessie.

It was Jessie, all right, but she came in too suddenly, out of control as if she had been shoved from behind. She sprawled on the hard-packed dirt with a grunt of pain.

Behind her, Esteban Corrales stepped into the barn, with half a dozen tough-looking vaqueros behind him. He held a long, coiled blacksnake whip in his hand.

★
Chapter 20

Jessie felt a tremor go through her as she lay on the floor of the stable at Corrales's feet. It was not a shudder of fear, however, but a quiver that betrayed the depth of her anger. Corrales and the vaqueros had jumped her when she was almost to the barn, a few steps away from freedom. The frustration of it was almost more than she could stand.

A second later, she felt another tremor, but this one came from the ground on which she lay.

"Lupe, Lupe, Lupe," Corrales said, shaking his head. He let the whip uncoil, and it slithered onto the ground with a hiss, almost like the reptile for which it was named. "You disappoint me, *hermano*. I have given you so much, and this is how you repay me."

Lupe started toward his brother, hands outstretched in front of him as he pleaded, "You do not understand, Esteban! I was merely testing these prisoners, to see how treacherous they might be—"

"The only treacherous one is you, fool!" Corrales's hand lashed out with the whip, and it cracked wickedly, the sound echoing in the high-ceilinged stable. Lupe screamed and staggered back, pressing a hand to the gash on his cheek that had been opened up by the whip. "Did you think you could fool me?" Corrales went on. "You great, fat, stupid

169

piece of dung! I knew you were up to something. It was merely a matter of keeping an eye on you until I discovered what it was. When Juanita told me some ridiculous lie about Señorita Starbuck being sick, I knew that you were all conspiring against me!"

As blood welled between Lupe's fingers from the cut on his face and he sobbed wretchedly in pain and fear, Jessie rolled over and pushed herself to her feet. She glared at Corrales and said, "Juanita had nothing to do with this! If you hurt her, so help me—"

"The girl is unharmed," Corrales said coldly. "I will deal with her later. For now—Señor Ryan, put down that gun, or I will have my men shoot Señorita Starbuck!"

Ryan hesitated, obviously torn by the almost irresistible urge to lift the pistol and put a bullet through Corrales's brain. But even if he succeeded, the vaqueros would simply gun down all of them. Jessie could see the indecision warring on his rugged features.

"Put down the gun, Silencio," she said quietly. There might still be a way out of this, she thought.

"Ah, Jessica, you are showing some good sense at last," Corrales said. "Will you do as she says, Señor Ryan?"

Slowly, the big redhead stooped over and placed the gun on the ground.

Corrales snapped his fingers and gestured to his men. Several of them started toward Ryan.

"Not him," Corrales said sharply. "Although I am wounded deeply by the way Señorita Starbuck and Señor Ryan have abused my hospitality, I still have uses for both of them." He paused, looking at Lupe, then said, "Take my brother, instead."

"Noooo!" Lupe howled. The vaqueros closed in around him, grabbing him by the arms. They dragged him over in front of Corrales.

170

"Bare his back and tie him to that post," Corrales ordered.

Lupe screamed and whimpered as the vaqueros ripped his jacket and shirt from him. They hauled him over to one of the thick wooden columns that supported the roof of the stable. Using rawhide thongs from the tack room, they lifted his arms above his head and lashed his wrists to the beam.

Corrales moved the whip back and forth idly. It rustled in the dirt.

"First you, Lupe, then those two fools who drank the tequila you brought them. You see, I overheard you bragging before we came in."

"No, Esteban, you don't understand!" Lupe pleaded desperately. "I would never betray you! Never!"

"Save your lies, *gordo*." Corrales brought his arm back. "And save your breath for the screaming."

The whip shot forward.

Jessie and Ryan both flinched as the blacksnake curled across Lupe's broad, bare back and then leaped away with a crack, leaving behind a thin line of blood. Lupe shrieked and surged against the post to which he was bound, but there was nowhere for him to go, no place to hide. No matter how much he squirmed, he could not pull free.

The whip cracked again and again.

"I will flay every inch of skin from your back, you fat lump of shit!" Corrales grated between clenched teeth. His breath was coming fast and harsh now as he slashed at his brother with the long whip. Lupe sobbed and moaned and screamed, horrible cries that tore from his throat with all the agonies of hell behind them.

Jessie and Ryan looked at each other, both of them thinking the same thing. How much longer could they stand by and watch this torture without doing something?

171

— even if interfering with Corrales would probably get them killed.

The whip rose and fell again, and suddenly Ryan stepped forward, ignoring the barrels of the pistols that the vaqueros turned toward him. "That's enough!" Ryan said raggedly. "*Madre de Dios,* that's enough!"

Corrales half turned, his face dark with fury. "If he takes another step, shoot him!"

The whip sprang forward again to lay its bloody caress across Lupe's back.

Ryan tensed, his big hands clenching into knobby-knuckled fists.

"Silencio, no!" Jessie said. The vaqueros cocked their pistols.

Outside, all hell broke loose.

Ki had reached the floor of the valley and was running toward the big house when he heard the shots. Perez had already launched the attack, Ki knew. He didn't waste any breath or energy on cursing. Instead he redoubled his pace until he was running as fast as he dared on unfamiliar ground in the dark. He relied on his keen eyesight and the mysterious inner sense that had always served him well to pick up any obstacles he would need to dodge.

Volley after volley of gunfire rang out, filling the night. It sounded like a small war up there, Ki thought.

In a matter of minutes, he hoped, he would be joining that war. . . .

Corrales spun around, as startled as anyone else in the barn by the unexpected storm of gunfire outside. He shouted orders in Spanish at his men, who turned and ran to the entrance of the stable. They dashed outside, guns ready. Their pistols began to bang crazily. Men shouted and cursed, and the thunder of hoofbeats filled the air.

Ryan dove for the pistol he had placed on the ground earlier.

Some instinct must have warned Corrales. He whirled and lashed out with the whip again. This time the blacksnake coiled around Ryan's wrist just as the big redhead scooped up the gun. Corrales jerked on the whip at the same instant as Ryan squeezed the trigger. The bullet whined off harmlessly, Ryan's aim ruined by the bloody gash the whip cut in his wrist. The gun slipped from his fingers and fell to the ground again.

Corrales yanked a small pistol from the sash around his waist. "I do not know what is going on out there, but it appears I must kill you now, Señor Ryan!" he said.

Before he could pull the trigger, Jessie leapt at him from the side. The heel of her boot caught him on the arm as she kicked high. The pistol went spinning out of Corrales's grasp, unfired.

Jessie landed a little off balance and had to go to one knee to catch herself. As she did, another tremor ran through the ground. This time, the noise that accompanied it was loud enough to drown out for a moment all the chaos outside the barn. Corrales's head snapped up, and he gasped, "El Monte del Fuego!"

The trembling eased for a few seconds, then a fresh wave of it rolled through the earth. The rumbling sound grew louder and louder. Juanita dashed through the open doors of the barn, crying, "The Mountain of Fire! It explodes!"

A man on horseback suddenly bulked in the entrance behind her. Jessie saw his ugly face and the single bandolier across his barrel chest, and even though she had not gotten a look at the man in Monterrey, she knew this had to be Lucardo Perez. There was a pistol in Perez's hand, and it belched smoke and flame as he fired.

The bullet caught the running Juanita in the back and pitched her forward. Perez urged his horse on, its hooves barely missing the wounded girl as she rolled out of the way. The eyes of the *bandido* looked toward the stall where Lucifer reared and whinnied shrilly, spooked by everything that was going on. Perez shouted, "Ah, there is my horse!"

Ryan was back on his feet, grabbing Jessie and pulling her to the side, out of the line of fire. Corrales shouted, "How dare you, you filthy bandit!" He flicked the whip toward Perez.

Perez moved with surprising speed, throwing up his free hand and catching the whip. He lifted his gun with the other hand, cocking it as he brought the yawning black muzzle to bear on Corrales.

The lantern light in the barn glinted on something shiny as it flew through the air, coming from the entrance. Perez cried out in pain, letting go of the whip and pawing futilely at his back as his other arm jerked the gun up and his finger pulled the trigger involuntarily. The bullet went high, well over the heads of everyone on the ground. Perez sagged forward, still trying to reach the thing imbedded in the middle of his back.

It was a razor-sharp throwing star, Jessie saw. A *shuriken*. Only one man she knew used those.

She saw him at the entrance of the barn.

"Ki!"

She started toward him as Perez turned his horse. The *bandido* tried to bring his gun to bear, but Ki's hand flickered again in a blur of motion, and this time Perez sagged backward in the saddle. He dropped his gun and brought both hands to his throat, brushing his fingers over the *shuriken* that was almost invisible, so deeply had it sunk into the folds of flesh beneath his beard. Blood suddenly welled from his mouth.

174

He pitched off the horse to land with a crash on the floor of the stable.

Jessie reached Ki's side and threw her arms around him in a tight hug. "You are all right?" he asked over the continuing roar of the volcano coming fully awake at long last.

"I am now," she said.

There was no time for anything else. Several men on horseback swept toward the barn, firing as they came. Ki threw himself to the ground, dragging Jessie with him. The bullets sang over their heads.

Ryan appeared at their side. He had the gun in his hand again and, using his left hand to steady the injured right, he fired toward the riders. One of the men plunged from his saddle, and the others veered away.

"What the hell's going on?" Ryan asked as he lowered the pistol.

"Perez's men are attacking the ranch," Ki explained. "They want Lucifer."

"No one will take this horse!"

The angry voice came from Esteban Corrales. The trio near the doors turned to see him standing in front of the stall where Lucifer lunged back and forth, smashing against the stout wooden walls in his frenzy. Corrales had the little pistol in his hand again. He had dropped the whip. He pointed the gun at Jessie, Ki, and Ryan and went on, "You are all conspiring against me! You are in league with that bandit Perez! I will kill you, and then I will defend my rancho!"

He had gone completely around the bend, Jessie thought. But that didn't make him any less dangerous. Ki might be able to down him with a *shuriken,* or Ryan might shoot him, but Corrales was going to get at least a few shots off before he fell.

Or at least he would have if Lucifer hadn't suddenly bolted forward with all the strength in his large, powerful frame. The horse hit the gate at the front of the stall and smashed it open. Lucifer's shoulder and the debris from the shattered gate crashed into Corrales's back at the same time.

The madman was flung forward by the impact. He fell to his knees as the pistol spun away from him. Lucifer raced past him, free at last. Corrales screamed, "No! Come back here!" He scrambled after the gun on hands and knees.

But to reach it he had to go past the beam where his brother Lupe was tied, only half-conscious from the beating he had taken. Jessie saw Lupe's eyes blink in confusion, and then they focused suddenly on Corrales crawling past him. Lupe kicked backward as he sobbed.

The kick caught Corrales in the side and sent him tumbling over once. He cursed, righted himself, reached for the gun once again.

Shaking fingers closed over the butt of the weapon and picked it up before Corrales could get hold of it.

He looked up into the pale face of Juanita. Pain had etched lines into her features, and the back of her peasant blouse was sodden with blood from the gunshot wound Perez had inflicted on her. But as the ground shook crazily and the rumble of the volcano grew to be almost deafening, Juanita screamed over the sound, "You are to blame for this, Don Esteban! Your evil has brought the judgment of the spirits on this valley!"

"No!" Corrales cried. "Put that gun down, Juanita!"

"I loved you, Don Esteban." Her voice was softer now, and she did not know if anyone heard her or not. It no longer mattered. "You turned me away, but I always loved you."

Then darkness enfolded her as she pressed the trigger.

Jessie turned her face away and pressed it into Ryan's

chest as the bullet bored through Corrales's skull, bursting out the back of his head in a shower of brains, blood, and shattered bone.

Beside Jessie and Ryan, Ki had hold of Lucifer's mane. He had caught it as the black stallion tried to rush past them. Now he tightened his grip as he looked with grim satisfaction at the motionless bodies of Corrales and Perez. The two men responsible for so much death and bloodshed had finally paid the ultimate price for their crimes.

"If that volcano really is erupting, we've got to get out of here!" Ki reminded Jessie and Ryan.

"Hang on to Lucifer," Ryan said. "I'll get El Rey and some other horses!"

As he hurried through the stable, flinging open the gates of the stalls so that the frantic horses would at least have a chance to escape the horror that was coming, Jessie ran over to the post where Lupe was still tied. She plucked the *shuriken* from Perez's back and used the keen edge of the deadly little weapon to slash the rawhide thongs binding Lupe to the beam. He sagged and almost fell as his arms dropped.

"Come on, Lupe!" Jessie urged. "We've got to get out!"

"Where . . . where is Emiliano?" he panted.

Jessie's mouth tightened. "In the house, tied up in his room. I ran into him when I was sneaking out of the house. But there's no time to go get him!"

"He is *mi hermano*! I have to save him!"

"He wouldn't do that for you!" Jessie said vehemently.

"N-no," Lupe panted. "He would not. But I am not him." He staggered toward the entrance, almost all of his back a raw, gaping wound where Corrales had flayed him with the blacksnake.

Ryan came up beside Jessie, leading El Rey and two more horses. He hadn't taken the time to do more than put halters on the animals. They would have to ride bareback when they fled. Ryan was holding another halter for Lucifer.

"Let's go," the big redhead shouted. "That damned mountain's going to blow its top any minute!"

That was true, Jessie figured. The way the ground was shaking, an eruption was imminent.

Ki took the spare halter and slapped it on Lucifer, then reached for one of the other horses. "You must ride Lucifer, my friend," he told Ryan. "Jessie will take El Rey, and I will ride one of these other horses."

Ryan nodded curtly. That made the most sense considering the weights of all of them and the fact that Lucifer was most comfortable with Ryan on his back.

Ki looked around. Jessie was on one knee beside Juanita, a couple of fingers pressed to the neck of the maid. Jessie looked up and shook her head grimly.

"I figured she was gone," Jessie said as she stood up and reached for El Rey's reins. "But I had to make sure before we left."

"Watch out when we leave the stable!" Ryan said as he swung up onto Lucifer's back. "Corrales's men and those *bandidos* could still be trading shots."

Ki helped Jessie onto El Rey, then mounted one of the other horses and led the remaining animal. When they rode out of the barn, they saw only a few bodies scattered on the ground. No one was moving. It looked as if Corrales's vaqueros and Perez's *bandidos* had all taken off for the tall and uncut when the Mountain of Fire began shaking and spitting fire.

Jessie couldn't blame them for that. Instead of a red glow in the sky above the peak, the entire heavens seemed to be ablaze tonight. As she looked up at the mountain, the largest explosion yet shook the earth like a cat shaking a mouse. Flames shot high into the air above the peak, and liquid fire seemed suddenly to overflow it.

"Lava!" Ki exclaimed. "If we can reach the floor of the valley, we can probably outrun it!"

Jessie turned El Rey toward the big house. "Lupe!" she shouted at the top of her lungs, knowing the effort was futile but having to make it anyway. "Lupe!"

Ryan reached over and caught her arm. "He can't hear you! We've got to go, Jessie!"

She knew he was right. She hated to leave Lupe behind. He had tried, at long last, to oppose his brother's evil. But he had also made his own choice to go back into the house in search of his other brother.

A spasm of coughing gripped Jessie. The air seemed to be filling with ashes and a stench like brimstone. The gases spewed out by a volcano could be as dangerous as the lava, she recalled reading. She whirled El Rey and dug her heels into the flanks of the big roan, heading him down the slope away from the house. Ki and Ryan followed her example. Ki was still leading the extra horse.

He was about to let go of its reins when a small figure came running out of the shadows calling his name. He recognized Ana and slowed his mount long enough to bend over and scoop her up into his arms.

"I was afraid," she said in answer to his unasked question, practically shouting even though her mouth was close to his ear. "When El Monte del Fuego began to speak, I came to look for you!"

Ki was glad she had. She might have been safe in the spot where he had left her, but there was no way of being sure about that. "Can you ride?" he asked.

Ana nodded, and he brought both horses to a stop. She transferred to the other one with his help, then they galloped after Jessie and Ryan. The horses Ki and Ana rode were not as good as Lucifer and El Rey, of course, but they

179

were some of Corrales's fine, blooded stock, and they were fast, strong creatures. The four riders raced as fast as they dared down the side of the mountain.

But when Jessie glanced over her shoulder, she saw to her horror that the lava flow already covered the upper half of the mountain, and it was hissing and leaping toward them, coming closer with every passing second. When it reached the valley floor, it would slow down some, and the four puny humans might stand a chance then.

If they got there first. . . .

Lupe Corrales staggered out of the hacienda, his brother Emiliano's arm draped across his shoulders. Lupe knew he couldn't go much farther. His heart was pounding madly, and it felt as if there were a broad band of some sort stretched across his chest, drawing tighter with each moment that went by. His left arm hung useless as pains shot up it. Not only that, but he was weak and dizzy from loss of blood.

He was dying, and he knew it.

"Run, Emiliano," he murmured as he stumbled to a halt. "Save yourself."

"Nonsense," Emiliano said, lifting his voice so that he could be heard over the rumbling, which was dying away now. But it was being replaced by other sounds—the crackle of flames as pine trees ignited like torches, the roar of massive boulders tumbling down the mountainside as they were shaken from perches where they had sat for hundreds of years, the gigantic hiss of the lava flow that was like the voice of a thousand angry snakes—all of them blended into a hideous medley of destruction.

Lupe pushed weakly at his brother's shoulder. "Go, please go . . ." Then he slumped to his knees, doubling over as a fresh burst of pain exploded inside his chest.

"And miss the opportunity to study an eruption such as

this?" Emiliano shook his head and patted his brother on the shoulder. "No, I will stay." He raised his gaze to the wall of lava that was nearly upon them and murmured, "Fascinating . . ."

An instant later, the lava swept over the house, smashing it utterly and burning everything that would burn. The liquid fire took the two pitiful figures with it as it continued its inexorable plunge down the mountain.

They had almost reached the floor of the valley. Jessie looked back again and witnessed the destruction of the house. She thought for an instant that she saw a couple of tiny shapes silhouetted against the hellish glare of the lava, then decided her eyes had been playing tricks on her. She turned her attention back to the desperate race for life being played out in this once-beautiful valley. Now fires were burning everywhere they looked, and the heat was so awful that Jessie felt as if she herself were about to burst into flames.

"Come on!" Ryan urged. "We can make it!"

The lava flow seemed to pick up even more speed as it reached the lower slopes of the mountain. Jessie could almost feel it lapping at her heels. That was an illusion, she knew. If the lava had really been that close, she and the others would all have been dead by now. She realized suddenly that the horses were straining forward over flat ground. They had made it to the floor of the valley.

So had the lava, but as it reached the base of the mountain, it began to spread out, and its forward progress slowed dramatically. Jessie looked back again. They were going to make it, she thought. They were going to make it!

But none of them slowed down, not yet.

They wanted to put this fire as far behind them as they could.

★

Chapter 21

Jessie tossed the copy of the San Antonio newspaper onto the bed beside her and snorted in disgust. "Minor geological disturbance, my ass!" she said. "That was a volcano, and the damn thing blew its top off!"

Silencio Ryan grinned. "You know that, and I know that, and Ki knows that . . . but face it, Jessie, all that happened in an isolated valley in the middle of the Sierra Madre. Folks up here don't know what really happened—and they don't care, either."

"I know," Jessie said with a sigh. "But it seems like somebody ought to know the truth."

"Wouldn't do much good. It wouldn't bring back that girl Juanita, or that hombre Wayland who helped Ki, or Lupe Corrales. And they were the only decent folks who didn't make it out down there."

"Along with all those people Corrales's men killed on the train," Jessie reminded him.

Ryan nodded solemnly. "You're right. But nothing's going to bring them back, either."

She snuggled against him, enjoying the feel of his brawny arm as it went around her and pressed her tightly to his side. Since both of them were naked as the day they were born, that closeness soon had some inevitable consequences.

Jessie reached under the sheet to caress his erection. As she ran her fingers lightly along the shaft, she said, "I suppose you have to go back to Don Arturo's hacienda, don't you?"

"Sooner or later," Ryan replied with a grin. "But not right away. I already sent him a wire letting him know we ran into some trouble. Told him everything was all right now but not to expect me back for a while."

Everything *was* all right now, Jessie supposed. As all right as the memories were going to let them be for a while. She and Ryan were sharing a room in the best hotel in Laredo, and Ki and Ana were in another room right down the hall. Lucifer and El Rey and the other two horses they had brought with them were all stabled nearby, being pampered as befitted such prize animals. Jessie planned to take all of them back to the Circle Star with her.

They had ridden out of the Sierra Madre, following the spur line back to the main tracks of the railroad. Another northbound train had come along within a day, and they had flagged it down. The story of the raid on the train had already spread far and wide, and the railroad company regarded Jessie, Ki, and Ryan as heroes once they heard how justice had caught up to Esteban Corrales and Lucardo Perez. Nothing was too good for them. The railroad was paying for the hotel rooms here in Laredo, in fact, along with caring for the horses.

During the journey, Ki explained how he had come to still be alive when Jessie had been halfway convinced— even though she didn't want to admit it—that he was dead. It was a fantastic story, and she had promised Ki that they would return to the lonely jacal in the foothills and put up a decent marker on Timothy Wayland's grave. Ki liked that idea. He could take Ana back to her family at the same time.

Unless, of course, she decided that she wanted to come to the Circle Star and work in the big ranch house there.

That was an offer Silencio Ryan would never accept, Jessie knew. The big redhead valued his independence, and his relationship with Don Arturo Hernandez, too much to give up either one of them. Jessie could understand that. But understanding didn't mean that she wouldn't miss Ryan once they went their separate ways.

She would just have to make the most of the time between now and then, she told herself. She scooted around, swung a leg over Ryan's midsection, and lowered herself onto his erect shaft.

"Lord, woman, you're shameless!" Ryan grinned up at her. "We haven't even gone down for breakfast yet this morning."

"That's a good reason to work up an appetite," Jessie said as she placed her palms on his chest to balance herself and began pumping her hips up and down. She closed her eyes as she felt him swelling inside her.

This was one eruption she was looking forward to.

If you enjoyed this book, subscribe now and get...

TWO FREE

A $7.00 VALUE—

If you would like to read more of the very best, most exciting, adventurous, action-packed Westerns being published today, you'll want to subscribe to True Value's Western Home Subscription Service.

Each month the editors of True Value will select the 6 very best Westerns from America's leading publishers for special readers like you. You'll be able to preview these new titles as soon as they are published, *FREE* for ten days with no obligation!

TWO FREE BOOKS

When you subscribe, we'll send you your first month's shipment of the newest and best 6 Westerns for you to preview. With your first shipment, two of these books will be yours as our introductory gift to you absolutely *FREE* (a $7.00 value), regardless of what you decide to do. If you like them, as much as we think you will, keep all six books but pay for just 4 at the low subscriber rate of just $2.75 each. If you decide to return them, keep 2 of the titles as our gift. No obligation.

Special Subscriber Savings

When you become a True Value subscriber you'll save money several ways. First, all regular monthly selections will be billed at the low subscriber price of just $2.75 each. That's at least a savings of $4.50 each month below the publishers price. Second, there is never any shipping, handling or other hidden charges—*Free home delivery*. What's more there is no minimum number of books you must buy, you may return any selection for full credit and you can cancel your subscription at any time. A TRUE VALUE!

A special offer for people who enjoy reading the best Westerns published today.

WESTERNS!

NO OBLIGATION

Mail the coupon below

To start your subscription and receive 2 FREE WESTERNS, fill out the coupon below and mail it today. We'll send your first shipment which includes 2 FREE BOOKS as soon as we receive it.